IMPEACH SCREECH!

"Saved by the Bell" titles include:

Mark-Paul Gosselaar: Ultimate Gold
Mario Lopez: High-Voltage Star
Behind the Scenes at "Saved by the Bell"
Beauty and Fitness with "Saved by the Bell"
Dustin Diamond: Teen Star

▲   ▼   ▲

Hot new fiction titles:

Zack Strikes Back
Bayside Madness
California Scheming
Girls' Night Out
Zack's Last Scam
Class Trip Chaos
That Old Zack Magic
Impeach Screech!
One Wild Weekend

IMPEACH SCREECH!

by Beth Cruise

Collier Books
Macmillan Publishing Company *New York*
Maxwell Macmillan Canada *Toronto*
Maxwell Macmillan International
New York Oxford Singapore Sydney

Collier Books
Macmillan Publishing Company
866 Third Avenue
New York, NY l0022

Maxwell Macmillan Canada, Inc.
l200 Eglinton Avenue East
Suite 200
Don Mills, Ontario M3C 3N1

Macmillan Publishing Company is part of the Maxwell Communication
Group of Companies.
Printed in the United States of America

l0 9 8 7 6 5 4 3 2 1

ISBN 0-02-042762-X

To
Screech fans
everywhere.

Chapter 1

▲ ▼ ▲ ▼ ▲

Zack Morris impatiently drummed his fingers on his favorite table at his favorite hangout. The Max was jammed full of laughing, talking, shouting Bayside High students. Zack surveyed the crowd and then turned to his friends.

"They have a lot of nerve," he said disgustedly. "Who said all these kids could show up at *my* place?"

Kelly Kapowski laughed, tossing a lock of silky dark hair out of her eyes. "I didn't know they renamed this place the Zack instead of the Max," she said teasingly.

"You don't understand, Kelly," Zack said to his girlfriend. "I'm starving. We had a poison special for lunch today in the cafeteria."

"It was a health food special," Jessie Spano corrected. Jessie was always the one to point out the facts. She had a terrific brain cooking underneath a gorgeous exterior.

"Same thing," Zack declared. "That lentil casserole looked like it was dredged up from a swamp."

"That's why the Max is so crowded," Kelly said. "Everyone can't wait to indulge in some serious junk food."

"No matter what it does to our hips," Lisa Turtle groaned. But Lisa had nothing to worry about. She was a pretty African-American teen who hated exercise but always stayed slim. It was lucky, because she was totally obsessed with clothes.

"Personally, I think Mr. Belding made a big mistake when he hired the new head of the cafeteria staff," A. C. Slater joined in. He shook his curly, dark head. "I heard that Ms. Meadows used to run a health food store downtown."

"Not Fresh Meadow Foods?" Jessie asked. "That was my favorite store. Their tofu sandwich was out of this world."

Slater shuddered. "Out of this world is right. In my opinion, tofu should be sent into orbit."

"You're crazy," Jessie said. "I love health food."

"My idea of health food is a tomato on my bacon cheeseburger," Slater declared. He grinned at Jessie. They were total opposites, but they were nuts about each other. "Speaking of cheeseburgers, where's mine? I have football practice later, and I need red meat." He flexed a muscular arm. "You don't get *this* body from tofu, momma," he said to Jessie.

"I think all that red meat has petrified your brain," Jessie grumbled.

Kelly's long hair flew as she peered back toward the kitchen. "I think you're in luck, Slater. Here comes our order."

In another minute, the waitress had set down a tray loaded with juicy cheeseburgers for the gang, a tofu burger for Jessie, crispy french fries, and ice-cold sodas.

"Finally!" Zack said, rubbing his hands together in satisfaction. He picked up his cheeseburger, his mouth poised for that first, delicious bite.

But suddenly, Samuel "Screech" Powers burst into the Max, his frizzy curls bobbing and his elastic face transformed into a huge, goofy grin. He threw his arms wide and his head back.

"Thank you, Babette Neidermeyer, wherever you are!" he yelled.

"What is Screech yodeling about?" Zack asked the gang as Screech tried to wend his way to their table.

"I don't know," Slater said, "but if we wait to try to figure it out, we won't be eating until Friday." He took a big bite of his cheeseburger.

"Babette is the school treasurer," Jessie explained. "She's out with mono, though. Mr. Belding postponed the student council meeting today. That's why I could come to the Max." Jessie was president of the senior class and of a zillion other committees. Slater sometimes complained that she had more meetings than a Hollywood producer.

"But what does that have to do with Screech?" Zack asked.

"And where *is* Screech?" Lisa asked, scanning the crowd.

A group of basketball players who were waiting for a table suddenly parted, and Screech popped out from their tall midst like a cork. He landed in front of the gang's table on his size-ten purple, zebra-patterned sneakers.

Adjusting his striped suspenders, Screech slid into a seat. "Greetings from your newly fiscally minded friend," he said.

"Mr. Belding appointed *you* to take over Babette's job?" Jessie asked incredulously.

Screech nodded proudly. "That's right. He got the best man for the job."

Zack guffawed. "Screech, you need a calculator to tell time. How are you going to deal with all that accounting?"

"Hey, I've been preparing for this job all my life," Screech said earnestly. "Didn't I come in second in the Monopoly tournament at Camp Tegatonga?"

"You were eight years old," Slater pointed out.

Screech looked misty-eyed. He clapped a hand to his chest. "Even then, I knew."

"And you came in fifth," Zack corrected. "You went down in flames after you sold me Park Place and Broadway for two dollars and a Baby Ruth."

"So I've learned some things since then," Screech insisted. "I'm like a bull in a bear market. Or is it a bear in a bull market? Or a bullish bear in a super-market?"

"Never mind, Screech," Jessie said. "Accounting is not going to be your biggest problem. The class fund *is*. It's super low. If you don't think of something pronto, the senior class fund is going to be finito."

"No problemo," Screech said confidently.

"I know what being broke is like," Kelly said ruefully. "It's a permanent condition with me." Kelly came from a large family. Her parents worked hard, but they didn't have much money for extras.

"Well," Lisa said with a philosophical shrug, "so what if the class is a little broke? We'll just have to cut down on pep rally posters or something."

"It's more serious than that, Lisa," Jessie said, shaking her head. "The last I heard, the Friday night dance might have to be canceled. There's no money for a band or refreshments or decorations."

"This *is* serious!" Lisa exclaimed. "I just bought a new dress!"

Screech waved a hand. "Go ahead and break out that taffeta, Lisa. I've already solved the problem. After Saturday night, the debits will outnumber the assets—"

"You mean the assets will outnumber the deb-its," Jessie corrected. "At least, I *hope* that's what you mean."

"—and the operating budget will, uh, be full of legal blender." Screech crossed his arms in satisfaction.

Lisa rolled her eyes. "*Tender,* Screech."

"Gosh, Lisa, I think you're tender, too," Screech said, batting his eyes at Lisa. Even though Screech had finally found happiness dating Nanny Parker, he still carried a Statue of Liberty-size torch for Lisa.

"I'm talking about bills, Screech," Lisa said impatiently.

"You have a crush on two guys at once?" Screech asked incredulously. "And they're both named Bill? That's really something."

"No, you're really something," Lisa responded. "But what that something *is,* gives me nightmares."

Slater put down his cheeseburger. "Tell us how you're going to solve the cash fund problem, Screech."

"I had a brilliant idea that Nanny suggested," Screech explained. "I already told it to Mr. Belding, and he's all for it. A celebrity auction."

"Oooooo," Lisa said. "Celebrities? That sounds divine."

"You mean like movie stars?" Kelly asked doubtfully. "Or sports figures?"

"Well, maybe not movie stars," Screech said. "But actors, yeah. And definitely sports figures."

"Screech, what are you talking about?" Jessie asked suspiciously. "You don't know any celebrities."

"Sure I do," Screech said. "I know Zack, Lisa, and Slater, and Riley McGee, and Ms. Meadows."

"But they aren't celebrities," Jessie protested.

"Sure they are. They're Bayside High celebrities. And each of them has something someone would want. For example, Ms. Meadows offered to cook a romantic dinner for two."

"Great," Slater groaned. "Mashed yeast by candlelight."

"And Riley McGee offered to give someone a free acting lesson. He'll even tape the person on his video camera," Screech said. Riley McGee was the star of the Bayside Players.

"What about Slater?" Lisa asked.

"Yeah, Screech," Slater said. "What am I going to do?"

"Give someone your secret pointers on passing a football," Screech responded promptly. He turned to Lisa. "And I was hoping you'd offer to give someone a day at the mall for a fashion make-over."

"Cool," Lisa said approvingly. "Basically, *every* girl at Bayside could use my help."

"What about Zack?" Kelly asked.

"Well," Screech said, "I gave that a lot of thought. He *is* a track star. But his main claim to fame is something else."

Jessie grinned. "Is he going to give class-cutting lessons?"

"No, he's going to take someone out on a romantic date," Screech said. "Zack picks the time and the place."

"Far out!" Zack exclaimed. Then he caught Kelly's frosty look. "I mean, gosh; do I have to, Screech?"

"It's for the good of the school," Screech said.

"Wait a second," Kelly said to Screech. "I don't want girls bidding on my boyfriend. Go pick some single guy to raffle off, Screech."

"Kelly, Kelly, Kelly," Zack said, shaking his head. "Where's your school spirit? You're head cheerleader. How would it look if you didn't support Bayside?"

"I never thought of that," Kelly said in a small voice. She turned to Jessie. "What if a girl bids on Slater, Jessie? I mean, she might not care about football, but she might care about *him.*"

Jessie tossed her long, curly hair. "As far as I'm concerned, if another girl wants Slater, she's welcome to bid on him."

"Way to go, momma," Slater said, rubbing his hands.

"But if I don't *win* the bidding, she's going to be dead meat," Jessie finished.

"Gosh," Kelly said. "I'd love to bid on you, Zack, but I'm really broke. I don't get my paycheck from the Yogurt 4-U until next Saturday."

"Don't worry about it, Kelly," Zack said. "I'll just have to suffer through a date with some poor girl who craves my bod and is willing to pay for the privilege of being with it for an evening. It's a sacrifice I'll have to make for good ol' Bayside High."

"You're a real saint, Zack," Lisa observed sarcastically.

The waitress put their bill down on the table, and Jessie and Kelly began to figure out what everyone owed.

"I'm glad you're willing, Zack," Screech said. "Because Nanny told me that Cathie Lynn Carmody is saving up to bid on you."

Cathie Lynn was the nerdiest girl at Bayside High. Her glasses were about two feet thick, and her favorite topic of conversation was algebraic equations. Zack shot a glance at Kelly, but her dark head was bent over the bill, so she hadn't heard Screech.

Zack cleared his throat. "You know, Kelly, maybe you're right," he said, giving her his trademark oh-so-sincere look out of hazel eyes. "I shouldn't be in the auction. We're going steady, after all. I don't want to date anyone but you."

"Oh, Zack. You're so sweet," Kelly said with a sigh. "But I really think we're being selfish. After all, the senior class fund is at stake. You have to participate."

"But—"

Kelly's blue eyes twinkled. "And, besides, you don't want to disappoint Cathie Lynn, do you?"

Chapter 2

▲ ▼ ▲ ▼ ▲

That night, Kelly was so tired when she got home from work at the Yogurt 4-U that she could barely pick up her feet. She shuffled from her car to the front porch. She had a strawberry stain on her uniform and walnut crumbs under her fingernails. She had mashed banana in her hair and coconut flakes in her shoes. She felt like a giant fruit salad.

A long, hot shower was in order, but Kelly had barely gotten wet when the water turned cool, then freezing. She yelped and turned it off, and then reached for a towel, shivering.

Kelly toweled off, frowning. There were days when she thought that being part of a big family was the best thing in the world. Then there were days like this, when the hot water ran out at 8:00 P.M. and the Oreo package that had been full that morning held only a quarter of a cookie with all the white stuff scraped off. On those days, Kelly thought wistfully of what it would be like to be an only child.

Kelly padded down the hall and opened the door to her bedroom. Just this year, when her father had built an extra room over the garage for her brothers, she'd finally snagged a room of her own. But, as usual, her sister Nicki was sitting at Kelly's bureau, trying on her makeup. So much for privacy.

"Out," she said to Nicki.

"But—"

"No buts," Kelly said, pointing her finger to the hall. "I have to study."

Nicki sighed and started out.

"And leave my lipstick," Kelly ordered. "I paid six-fifty for it."

Pouting, Nicki slapped down the lipstick and went out. Kelly shut the door behind her. She stretched out on her bed and flipped open her textbook. She had a hot date with some French irregular verbs.

"*Dormir*," she read out loud. "To sleep. *Je dors, tu dors, il dort.* I sleep, you sleep...." She yawned. "He sleeps. *Nous dormons.* We all sleep. Ever-y-bod-y sleeeeeps...."

The next thing she knew, a hand was shaking her shoulder.

"Two vanilla with double sprinkles, coming up," she said sleepily.

"Kelly, sweetie, the phone is for you," her mom said gently. "Wake up."

Kelly rose and pushed her hair out of her eyes. "I'm awake, I guess. Who is it? Zack?"

Her mother's lips pressed together. "No. It's important, or I wouldn't have woken you. It's Marion Lenihan."

"Marion Lenihan?" Kelly asked in surprise. She had met Mrs. Lenihan in New York City during the senior class trip. Mrs. Lenihan was a snooty socialite who just happened to be distantly related to the Kapowskis. She had told Kelly in no uncertain terms that she had absolutely no interest in that branch of the family tree. Actually, she probably wanted to take a buzz saw to it, Kelly thought ruefully. The Kapowskis were about as far from classy as you could get. They were more hot dogs than caviar, that was for sure.

"What does she want?" Kelly asked, standing up and knotting the sash of her robe.

"Maybe I'd better let her explain," Mrs. Kapowski said. "You can take the call in our room."

This must be an occasion, Kelly thought as she followed her mother to her parents' room. She didn't have to talk on the hall phone and have six brothers and sisters crowding around trying to hear every word.

Her father was sitting on the edge of his arm-chair seat. He had such a serious expression on his face that Kelly felt a flutter of nerves. She picked up the bed-side phone.

"Hello?"

Marion Lenihan's haughty voice came through the receiver. "Is this Kelly?"

"Yes, it's me, Mrs. Lenihan."

"Well," Marion harumphed. "It's about time."

"I was sleeping. What's up?" Kelly asked. She wasn't about to be intimidated by Marion Lenihan.

"Oysters," Marion said.

"Excuse me?" Kelly said doubtfully. "I thought you said oysters."

"I did. I enunciate very clearly, Kelly, so you will always hear correctly. Oysters. Bad oysters. I had a dozen last night at La Normandie. I was never so sick in my life. I thought I would die. And I had a vision, Kelly. A vision of what the world would be like after I was gone. And do you know how it looked?"

"No, Mrs. Lenihan," Kelly said politely.

"Empty," Marion said flatly. "What am I leaving behind? Oh, there's the Lenihan Foundation, of course. And the wonderful Impressionist paintings I'm leaving to the Metropolitan Museum of Art. And, of course, the memory of *me*. But, suddenly, as wonderful as all that is, it isn't enough."

"Gosh," Kelly said. "I'm sorry."

"So I decided I needed an heir," Marion said. "A girl heir, preferably. And you're the only one I can think of."

Kelly's knees buckled, and she sank down on the bed. "Me?" she squeaked.

"Now, don't get excited yet, because I haven't decided for sure," Marion warned. "First of all, you're...unpolished. Unsophisticated. If you're going to carry on the Lenihan tradition, you must be an aristocrat. You must walk a certain way, talk a certain way, have that certain *je ne sais quoi*..."

"That what?" Kelly hadn't gotten that far in French class yet. Of course, it would help if she didn't fall asleep on her book every time she opened it.

"That indescribable something that I can't describe," Marion continued. "We need to groom you. Then I'll take a look at you and decide."

Kelly began to feel like a prize heifer. "Um, how do you intend to do that, Mrs. Lenihan?" she asked cautiously.

"Here's the plan," Marion said briskly. "Now, I assume that you attend some sort of dreadful public school, am I right?"

"I go to Bayside High, and it's a great school," Kelly said. "It's not dreadful at all."

"Mmmm, so you say. I want to enroll you in Miss Fopp's School for Young Ladies. It's an excellent school. My friend Missy Tremaine's daughter, Buffy, went there. It's in Los Angeles, but let's not hold that against it, shall we? Now, I called the headmistress and she's agreed to take you on. You can transfer there starting Monday. Agreed?"

"Wait a second," Kelly said. "Can't I have a few days to think about this?"

"Think about what, Kelly? Whether you want to inherit a fabulous fortune and have me as a benefactor or not?" Marion gave a chilly laugh. "Let's get real, as you kids say."

"But I don't want to leave my friends at Bayside," Kelly said.

"Oh, for heaven's sake, you can still see your little public school friends if you like. On weekends. Though I'm sure that once you get to know the *right* people, you won't be interested in those...bumpkins anymore."

"Hey, wait a second—" Kelly started.

"Once you're at Miss Fopp's for a period of time, we can talk about the proper college to attend. I'm thinking Smith or Wellesley, of course. But we can discuss that when the time comes. Now, details. First, you can now call me Aunt Marion. Second, I realize the social life at Miss Fopp's is competitive. You'll need to have money for things. I'm sending you my old charm bracelet and a pearl necklace, and I expect you to wear them. We'll start you out on an allowance of fifty dollars a week."

Kelly felt dizzy. Fifty dollars a week *and* Mrs. Lenihan would pay for college? She would never have to dump bananas on frozen yogurt ever again, Kelly fantasized dreamily. She wouldn't even have to *look* at yogurt ever again.

"Kelly? Are we agreed?"

Kelly looked down at her hands. She had broken two nails at work tonight. Her hair still smelled faintly of bananas, since there hadn't been enough hot water to wash it. Her feet were slightly swollen from standing on them for five hours. And tomorrow night, she'd have to do it all over again.

"Okay, Aunt Marion," she said slowly. "We're agreed."

▲   ▼   ▲

Over the next few days, Kelly found it hard to keep her secret. She was bursting to tell Zack, but every time she started to open her mouth, she shut it again. She was so confused. Of course, it was an incredible stroke of luck that Aunt Marion wanted to take charge of her education. But Kelly didn't really *like* her, and she felt guilty accepting the money.

"Sweetie, you might as well give it a try," her mother told her when Kelly expressed her doubts. "You know that your father and I want to send all you kids to college. We just can't afford it. This is an incredible opportunity for you. And if Marion helps you, maybe you can help your brothers and sisters. That's the way it works."

But leaving Bayside would be the hardest thing Kelly had ever done in her life. When she told Mr. Belding, he said he was sorry to see her go but realized it was a fantastic opportunity. And he would keep her secret until she decided to tell her friends.

Her friends...Kelly sighed as she took her outfit out of the closet for the Friday night dance. This would be her last dance as a Bayside student! She would miss graduation and the senior prom. She'd been through almost four years of fun and hard times at Bayside, and she'd end up graduating with strangers instead of her friends.

Kelly slipped on her silky blue tank top and

matching sarong skirt. She brushed her hair until it shone. She stared into the mirror, and tears filled her eyes. She would miss Bayside so much! She had been with Zack and Jessie and Slater and Lisa and Screech every single day for what seemed like forever. She couldn't imagine not suffering through classes with them and meeting at their lockers and throwing spitballs in study hall.

And Zack would really miss her, too, Kelly knew. He wouldn't want her to go to Miss Fopp's at all. Even the thought of missing their regular Saturday night date bothered him. He kept moaning about having to take out Cathie Lynn tomorrow night and how much he'd miss being with Kelly. He made Kelly promise to stay up and wait so that they could have a cup of hot chocolate together after his date. Zack was so sweet.

How was she going to tell him the bad news?

▲　　▼　　▲

Screech had scheduled the celebrity auction at the very beginning of the dance. That way, he'd have plenty of time to total up the money they raised. And, besides, if he didn't pay the band first, they wouldn't go on.

The first "celebrity" was Mr. Loomis, the history teacher, who offered a ride in a hot-air balloon that he flew on weekends. Mr. Loomis blushed when Ms. McCracken, the new art teacher, bid the highest.

Everyone knew that wild-and-crazy McCracken had gotten buttoned-down Loomis into hot-air ballooning in the first place.

The auction continued through Riley McGee's acting lesson and Ms. Meadows's dinner party and a chance to be the lead singer for one song with Greg Tolan's band. After Vivian Mahoney bid twenty-five dollars for an afternoon with personal shopper Lisa Turtle and Alan Witkin bid thirty for Slater's football passing secrets, it was Zack's turn.

Kelly watched him mount the stage as Screech announced what a romantic date with Zack Morris would include: a walk on the beach at sunset, crab cakes at a window table at Louie's Grill, and a moonlight drive to Smuggler's Cove.

"Ten dollars," Kelly called to start the bidding.

"I hear ten dollars," Screech called. "Do I hear fifteen?"

"Fifteen," Daisy Tyler said, giggling.

"Twenty," Cathie Lynn called. Her eyes were misty behind her glasses as she gazed adoringly at Zack.

"Twenty-five," Kelly said.

Cathie Lynn looked nervous. "Twenty-six fifty," she said.

"Do I hear thirty?" Screech called. He waved his gavel.

"Thirty," Kelly called. It was way over her budget, but she really wanted to see Zack tomorrow night. It would be the perfect opportunity to tell him the news. She had to break it to him in the right way.

"Do I hear thirty-five?" Screech called. "No? Okay, thirty going once, twice—"

"Fifty dollars!" someone yelled from the back of the hall. A gasp went through the crowd.

Screech looked at Kelly, and she shook her head. If things with Marion didn't work out, she'd sure need that fifty dollars. Kelly twisted around and peered through the crowd, trying to see which girl had bid so much.

"That's fifty going once," Screech said, "twice, sold! To, uh..." He peered through the crowd. Zack was already standing on his tiptoes, trying to see who it was.

"Phyllis Ptowski!" Screech called.

Relieved, Kelly turned to look for the girl. Phyllis was a sweet person, but she was plump and a little bit on the nerdy side. Kelly giggled as she turned back and saw Zack's face. He was definitely not thrilled about having to spend Saturday night with Phyllis.

Suddenly, Zack's expression changed. His mouth dropped open, and then a goony grin spread over his face. Kelly looked over and saw Phyllis pushing through the crowd to give Screech her money. But this wasn't the Phyllis that Kelly knew. She'd lost weight. She was gorgeous! She was dressed in an eye-catching black miniskirt, black turtleneck, and silver chain belt. Her hair was cut in a new soft style, and her big brown eyes looked even prettier in a face with cheekbones.

Kelly turned back to Zack. He jumped off the platform with a jaunty spring and headed for Phyllis. He looked absolutely delighted as they began to talk.

This didn't look good. Fuming, Kelly walked over. As she came up, she overheard the last of their conversation.

"So I'll pick you up at seven tomorrow night," Zack said. "We'll have a blast."

"I'm looking forward to it, Zack," Phyllis said.

Zack watched Phyllis walk away. "Wow," he said under his breath.

"Hey," Kelly said. She tapped him on the shoulder. "Remember me?"

"Oh, Kelly. Hi." Zack didn't even meet her gaze. He was still staring after the newly transformed Phyllis Ptowski.

"So what time will you be over tomorrow night after your date?" Kelly asked pointedly. "I have something to talk to you about."

"Tomorrow night? Gee, Kelly, I don't know. Phyllis paid a lot for the date. I'd hate to disappoint her by taking her home early. We'll see each other Sunday afternoon at the beach. We can talk then."

Kelly's lips pressed together. "But everybody else will be there."

"Oh. Right. Well, I guess I'll see you Monday. We'll have lunch together. Just the two of us. Okay?"

Zack's gaze slid away from her. Kelly grabbed him by his collar and yanked his face forward. "No, you won't see me on Monday," she said crisply. "You can eat lunch with Phyllis Ptowski. Zack, I'm transferring out of Bayside!"

Chapter 3

▲ ▼ ▲ ▼ ▲

"Kelly, don't you think that's a little extreme?" Zack asked. "You don't have to transfer out of Bayside because of Phyllis."

Kelly blew out an exasperated breath, making her silky bangs ruffle. "I'm not doing it because of Phyllis, you jerk," she said. "I'm doing it because of a million dollars. Maybe more."

Zack grinned. "Whoa. Someone's going to *pay* you to transfer out of Bayside? It's Daisy Tyler, right? I knew she wanted to be captain of the cheerleading squad really bad, but this is ridiculous."

Kelly grimaced. "I'm serious, Zack." Quickly, she told him about her aunt's phone call. "So you see," she finished, "I really can't turn it down. It's not only good for me, but for my brothers and sisters, too. Not to mention my parents. It takes a big burden off of them.

But it's going to be really hard to leave Bayside—and you. We just have to be strong."

"Right," Zack said. "I wonder how much money Marion has, exactly."

"I'll be taking the bus to Miss Fopp's," Kelly said with a sigh. "We won't get to ride to school together anymore."

"Speaking of cars," Zack said, "I wonder if Marion will buy you one. We could pick it out together. Porsche convertibles are really cool."

"But I'll still come to the Max after school," Kelly said. "That won't change."

"Speaking of change," Zack said, "you'll have plenty in your pockets. If you save up, I bet we could go on a fabulous vacation together."

"Zack, have you heard anything I've been saying?" Kelly asked, annoyed.

"Are you kidding, Kelly?" Zack said. "I've heard every single word. When it comes to fabulous fortunes, my hearing is perfect."

"But aren't you going to miss me? I thought you'd be upset," Kelly said, her blue eyes troubled. "You're only thinking about the money."

Zack instantly zoomed back to earth from big-bucks paradise. He slipped his arms around Kelly. "Of course I'll miss you," he said. "You're my one and only. I don't know how Bayside is going to get along without you, Kelly."

With a contented sigh, Kelly snuggled into his arms. "Oh, Zack. I knew you only cared about me, not the money."

"I always swore that you were worth a million bucks, Kelly," Zack said dreamily. "But I never thought you'd prove me right!"

▲   ▼   ▲

Later that night, Screech couldn't believe what an incredibly successful tycoon he'd turned out to be. He counted the bundle of money over and over again in the hall outside the gym as Nanny, Zack, and Mr. Belding watched.

"Howard Hughes, move over," he chortled.

"That might be hard for him, Screech," Zack said. "He's dead."

"Oh, Screech," Nanny said, gazing over his shoulder at the fistfuls of cash, "you're so brilliant! You saved the senior class fund! I'm going to write an article about it."

"Now, now, Nanny," Screech said. "You know how I feel about publicity."

"Oh. Okay."

"I *love* publicity! Put me on the front page!" Screech crowed.

"I should ask you to take over *my* financial affairs, Screech," Mr. Belding said. "Mrs. Belding has been handling the bills since she's gone back to school for her accounting degree, and, yesterday, our credit cards were canceled."

"Whoa," Zack said. "Don't let Lisa hear that story. She'll cry all night."

"This is serious," Mr. Belding said. "I've got to straighten things out. Old Pete needs an operation, and the hospital won't accept my credit. Pete's an important part of our family."

"I hope you straighten it out, Mr. Belding," Screech said. He straightened his green plastic visor. "If you need any help, you know who to call."

Just then, the senior class hood Denny Vane strode in through the side door of the school. Actually, he wasn't a real hood. He just liked to think of himself as one. Dressed in a black leather jacket and jeans, he clumped down the hall with his cronies. Their heavy black boots hit the floor, making the lockers rattle alarmingly.

"Whoa, dweeb-face," Denny said when he saw Screech. Then he noticed Mr. Belding. "I mean, how are you doing, Samuel?"

Nanny pushed her glasses up her nose and peered at Denny. "Samuel just saved the senior class fund, so I'd be a little more polite, Denny. He made up the deficit and then some. We can have the Spring Frolic now."

"Whoa, the Spring Frolic," Denny said. "I wouldn't miss it for the world. But whatever will I wear?"

"That's enough, Denny," Mr. Belding said. "Shouldn't you boys be heading for the dance?"

"That's right, Mr. Belding, sir," Denny said. "We're looking forward to shaking our booty, as you old-timers would say."

"Uh, right," Mr. Belding said with a frown.

"Come on, Nanny," Screech said. "Let's go to the student council room to lock up the money."

"I'd better go find Kelly," Zack said.

Everyone started to move away at once, and everyone collided. Zack and Screech knocked heads. Even Mr. Belding bumped right into Denny. The chains on Denny's motorcycle jacket clanked and clanged as he steadied Mr. Belding so that he wouldn't fall.

"Whoa, sorry, Mr. B," Denny said.

"It's okay, Denny," Mr. Belding said.

Screech rubbed his frizzy curls. "Wow, Zack. You have a hard head."

"Are you okay, Zack?" Mr. Belding asked.

"Sure," Zack said. "No harm done."

"Thank goodness," Mr. Belding said.

Zack slipped his arm through Mr. Belding's. "Now, come on, Kelly. They're playing our song."

Throwing a wink at Screech and Nanny as he passed, Zack steered a still-protesting Mr. Belding toward the gym.

▲   ▼   ▲

Sunday dawned bright and beautiful. The sun shone in a cloudless blue sky, and a soft breeze stirred the leafy green trees in Kelly's backyard. If this were a normal Sunday, she'd be throwing her towel in her knapsack and bicycling to Palisades Beach. Instead, she was standing in front of her closet, throwing her hands up in despair.

What *did* one wear to the first day at Miss Fopp's, anyway? Until she got her gray uniform, Kelly would have to wear her own clothes. She was sure that the right outfit would be sophisticated and conservative. But Kelly was fond of soft pastels and cheerful prints. Every piece of clothing she had seemed to be pink or orange or blue or festooned with flowers.

Kelly sighed. If she made a bad impression the first day, she'd be typecast forever. She'd become every high school student's worst nightmare: a nerd.

The phone rang, and Kelly raced out into the hall to answer it before one of her brothers did. Zack hadn't called last night, and she was dying to hear about his date with Phyllis. But when she snatched it up, it turned out to be Lisa.

"Hey, girlfriend," Lisa said. "Jessie and I are heading for the beach. Do you need a ride?"

Kelly sighed. "Oh, Lisa, I can't. I'm having a fashion crisis like you wouldn't believe."

"What are you talking about?" Lisa said. "Just throw on a bathing suit and a pair of cutoffs. Even *I* don't worry about outfits at the beach."

"I'm talking about *tomorrow*," Kelly said. "I don't know what to wear to my first day at Miss Fopp's."

"That's right," Lisa said. "Jessie and I were just talking about how cool it was that you're going to that school. Hey, I thought you were supposed to wear a uniform."

"I am," Kelly explained. "I'm getting fitted for it

on Monday, and I probably won't get it until Wednesday. You know how crucial a wardrobe is, Lisa. This school is all *girls*. I could be completely destroyed within seconds of arrival."

"Brrrr," Lisa shuddered. "I see what you mean. Let me think...." Lisa was silent for a few moments. "Okay. Monday—that pleated navy skirt you got last year and never wore, with your white cotton sweater and navy flats. Tuesday—the ecru linen pants your mother bought you with the matching blazer, canvas oxfords, aubergine silk blouse—"

"Ecru? Aubergine?"

"Beige and purple," Lisa said with a sigh. "You really need a fashion refresher course every month or so, Kelly. Aubergine is *in*. Okay, Wednesday, just in case the uniform isn't ready—pink blazer, white T-shirt, pink-and-white-striped mini, same flats as Monday. Got it?"

"Wow," Kelly said. "You're incredible, Lisa. Thanks."

"Kid stuff," Lisa said. "Now that we've taken care of that, do you want us to pick you up, or are you going to the beach with Zack?"

Zack. Kelly frowned. "Uh, Lisa, do you happen to know if Jessie noticed what time Zack got home last night?" Jessie lived next door to Zack. Unluckily for Zack, that fact occasionally came in handy.

There was a long pause, and Kelly's heart skipped a beat. "Come on," she said. "Out with it."

"Weeell," Lisa said, "she did happen to hear his Mustang pull up around one o'clock."

"*One?*" Kelly practically shrieked. "He missed curfew for Phyllis?"

"Maybe they ran out of gas," Lisa said. But her voice lacked conviction.

"Zack only runs out of gas if he wants to," Kelly said icily. "And I know one thing for sure. They *didn't* run out of steam."

▲   ▼   ▲

Kelly had just returned to the blanket after her dip when Zack showed up. He was wearing sunglasses, so she couldn't see his expression. He waved to them in a friendly way and then plopped down on the blanket, yawning.

"Late night?" Jessie asked, shooting a look at Kelly.

"You said it," Zack groaned. Then he sat up quickly. "I mean, nah. It just *felt* like it. This past week was pretty rough. I had a science quiz and a term paper due. Killer."

"What time *did* you get in, Zack?" Kelly asked. She hid her face behind a curtain of hair as she brushed sand off her legs.

"Hmmm, let me think," Zack said. "It wasn't too early. And it wasn't too late."

"So was it juuuussst right?" Jessie asked.

Zack squirmed on the blanket. "I wouldn't say that. It was just...the time I got in, that's all."

"It must have been a dynamite date if you can't remember," Kelly said.

"D-dynamite?" Zack stammered. "Not at all, Kelly. It was boring. Whew. Can't believe I got through it. I mean, Phyllis is a nice kid. But she's, uh, a little immature."

Just then, Phyllis Ptowski arrived at the beach with her friend Chrissie Nolan. Chrissie was a tall, skinny girl with a long, mournful face. She shook out their blanket a few yards away from where the gang was sitting. Phyllis pulled off her T-shirt and stepped out of her gym shorts. She was wearing a tiny red bikini and looked stunning. A surfer walking by looked once, then twice, and walked straight into a garbage can.

Phyllis waved at Zack, and Zack gave a half-hearted wave back. Then she blew him a kiss.

"Really immature," Lisa said. "I know just what you mean."

Kelly shot Zack a furious look. "Nothing happened," Zack said. "I promise." He *had* enjoyed his date with Phyllis. She was really pretty, and she had definitely been willing to be kissed at Smuggler's Cove. But Zack had kept his distance. She was cool, but she wasn't Kelly.

"You don't have to look so sorry about it," Kelly answered.

Suddenly, a shower of sand made them sit up in annoyance. Screech had run up to them without anyone noticing, and he'd jumped into the middle of the blanket, his eyes wild.

"Screech!" Lisa yelled. "Watch out!"

"I'm sorry, Lisa," Screech said, sitting down with a bump. "But an awful thing has happened!"

"I know," Lisa said, peering at her sandwich. "You got sand in my tuna."

"Worse than that," Screech babbled. "Much, much, much worse. What am I going to do?"

"Calm down, Screech," Zack said. "I'm sure it can't be that bad. Does your lizard have a stomachache or something?"

"Even worse," Screech said wildly. "*I* do. The senior class cash fund has been stolen!"

Chapter 4

▲ ▼ ▲ ▼ ▲

"What?" Zack exclaimed.

"It isn't possible," Jessie said.

"Maybe you misplaced the money," Kelly suggested.

"A thief at Bayside!" Lisa breathed. "How exciting!"

Just then, Slater arrived. He dumped his knapsack on the blanket and looked at everyone. "What's exciting? What's going on?"

"I'm dead meat, that's what's going on," Screech moaned. "I'm going to be court-martialed!"

"You can't be court-martialed if you're not in the army, Screech," Slater said logically.

"Well, then, I'll be impeached!" Screech wailed.

"Screech, calm down and tell us what happened," Jessie urged. "How do you know that the class fund money has been stolen?"

"Because it's not there," Screech answered. "I locked it in the drawer in the student council room. Nanny was with me. I have the key, since I'm treasurer. I was supposed to put it in the bank on Monday. But I've been kind of nervous about leaving it in school all weekend, so I went there this morning to get it and take it home. It was gone!"

"Wait a second," Zack said. "Could anybody else have taken it for safekeeping?"

"I'm the only one with a key to the drawer," Screech said, shaking his head.

"This *does* sound awful," Jessie said, frowning.

"Did the lock look like it had been forced?" Slater asked.

Screech shook his head. "That's what was so weird. There was no sign of tampering on either the lock on the council room door *or* on the desk drawer."

"This is totally weird," Lisa said. "Who would know how to pick locks at Bayside? It has to have been an outside job."

"Lisa, you've been watching too much TV. You sound like Columbo," Kelly said with a laugh.

Screech shuddered. "Don't remind me. If you see a guy in a really gross raincoat walking on the beach, warn me. I don't want to go to jail!"

"It wasn't your fault," Kelly reassured him.

"Yes, it was," Screech insisted. "That money was my responsibility." Biting his lip, he looked down. "This was the first responsible job I ever had, and I blew it. I let Mr. Belding down. I let Nanny down. Everyone is going to hate me."

The gang exchanged glances. Screech was a wacky guy, but he was super sensitive. He'd be crushed if the entire senior class blamed him for letting the money get stolen. He might never get over it.

"No one is going to hate you, Screech," Zack said firmly. "Because no one is going to find out."

"Yes, they will," Screech mumbled. "I have to give Mr. Belding the deposit receipt on Monday. Once he knows, he'll fire me, and everyone will know why."

Zack shook his head. "You can stall Mr. Belding. He's weird, but he's an okay guy. Ask him not to say or do anything for a couple of days. Tell him you think you know who stole the money, but you need a chance to find out for sure. I'm sure he'll go for it. Take it from me—he's persuadable."

"But what will I do then?" Screech asked. "I don't know who stole the money!"

"No," Zack said, "but maybe you can find out. Especially if you have all of us to help you. We'll turn Bayside High inside out. We'll follow every lead and examine every clue. We'll find the thief!"

Screech looked at the gang. "You'd do that for me?"

"You bet," Zack said, and everyone nodded agreement.

"Will you guys promise not to tell Nanny?" Screech asked. "She thinks I'm big man on campus now. This will crush her."

"We promise," Zack said. "Nanny won't find out."

"Don't worry, Screech," Jessie said. "Together, we can do anything."

Kelly nodded with the others, but she felt left out. There wasn't much sleuthing she could do over at Miss Fopp's. Over Jessie's head, she saw Phyllis Ptowski glance at Zack before heading slowly down to the water.

Kelly frowned. One of her best friends was in trouble, and a gorgeous girl had her sights on Zack. Kelly couldn't have picked a worse time to leave Bayside High if she tried!

▲   ▼   ▲

On Monday morning, Kelly nervously fingered Marion Lenihan's borrowed pearls as the bus approached her stop. She felt like jumping off the bus and running back to Palisades. Instead, she watched an exclusive suburb of Los Angeles pass by her window on the way to a school she didn't want to attend.

All her life, she had gone to school with her friends. She had met Lisa in kindergarten and Zack and Jessie in first grade. Screech's mother had baby-sat for the two of them when they were five years old. She had grown up surrounded by friends who knew her and loved her. From grade to grade, she could always count on them. And now, every day she would be surrounded by strangers.

Don't be silly, Kelly, she told herself. *They won't be strangers for long. I'm good at making friends, aren't I? I like people and like meeting new friends. I should look at this as an adventure.*

The bus trundled by a gorgeous brick mansion with white pillars.

Groups of girls stood outside in light gray skirts, white blouses, and gray blazers. At the end of a long, curving drive, Kelly glimpsed a parking lot that was full of expensive foreign sports cars. Kelly checked the sign chiseled in stone over the front steps. It was Miss Fopp's School for Young Ladies.

The city bus creaked to a halt half a block farther on, and Kelly got off. Smoothing her skirt anxiously, she started for the front walk. She was supposed to head straight for Miss Adelaide Rumson's office. Miss Rumson was really a principal, but she was called a headmistress here. The original Miss Fopp had died back in the forties. Miss Rumson was Miss Fopp's grandniece.

She walked past groups of girls who were talking and laughing in front of the school. Kelly thought longingly of Bayside. There, she'd be called and waved to as she moved through the crowd to join Zack and her friends. Here, girls gave her a quick up-and-down look and then turned back to their friends. Nobody even smiled at her. But then again, Kelly thought, to be fair, nobody would go out of their way to greet a stranger at Bayside, either. Maybe later, when she was in class or in the cafeteria, people would be more friendly.

Right by the front steps, a crowd of girls was listening intently to a tall girl who was talking quietly. Her blond hair reached to her waist, and thick bangs framed her narrow face. She wasn't beautiful, Kelly thought, but there was something about her that was stunning.

The girl wore an intricate necklace of strands of silver beads. Matching silver bracelets were wound around each wrist. Even though she wore the same uniform as the other girls, somehow it looked more stylish on her. A big silver pin on the back of her blazer gathered the material so that the jacket fit her waist snugly. She wore black tights with her black boots. Lisa would approve, Kelly thought, grinning. This girl had style.

The blonde was speaking in a low, intense voice, and Kelly couldn't catch what she was saying. Then, the crowd of girls all burst out laughing. The girl took a tiny step backward, her mouth twisted in a smile.

Encouraged by the laughter, Kelly decided that this tall blond girl must be nice. She walked up to her.

"Excuse me," she said. "Can you tell me where Miss Rumson's office is?"

The blonde swiveled. Her glittering green eyes flicked over Kelly. "You'll have to go to the reception desk first. It's the third door on the left down the front hall."

"Thanks. It's my first day," Kelly confessed.

"I'll alert the media," the girl said dryly. The rest of the crowd laughed, and Kelly felt her face flush. She couldn't tell if the girl was making fun of her or not.

"What's your name?" the girl asked. She had a look in her eye of a cat playing with a mouse, but Kelly decided she was probably being paranoid.

"Kelly Kapowski."

"Kapowski?" the girl repeated. She licked her lips as though Kelly were a nice, plump mouse and she was ready to pounce. Then, her glittering gaze roamed around the crowd of girls. "Well," she drawled, "how about that. I've never met a *Kapowski* before."

Kelly felt confused. Was the girl making fun of her or not? She couldn't be, Kelly decided. She didn't even know Kelly. Why should she want to make her uncomfortable on her very first day?

"What's your name?" Kelly asked in a friendly way.

The girl tossed her hair over a shoulder. "Suki Ballard."

"Suki?" Kelly frowned. "Gee, how about that. I never met a Suki before."

Suddenly, Kelly realized that she had used the very same words Suki had. It looked like she'd been making fun of her! A titter went through the group of girls, but with one look from Suki, it stopped.

"Didn't I see you get off the bus?" she asked Kelly.

Kelly nodded. "I live in Palisades."

"You don't have a car?" Suki asked in an incredulous tone.

"No," Kelly said.

"Oh," Suki said in a dismissing way. She turned back to her friends. "Let us know if you get lost, Kapowski," she tossed over her shoulder. "Here at Miss Fopp's, we believe in hospitality."

But she spoke in a flip, sarcastic tone, and Kelly felt her face flush again. Slowly, Kelly walked away. She'd really started off on the wrong foot.

As she gave her name to the frazzled-looking woman at the reception desk, Kelly told herself to chill out. So what if she'd annoyed one of the girls at Miss Fopp's? It probably wasn't any big deal. There were plenty of girls here to make friends with. It wasn't like Suki Ballard ran the school....

▲   ▼   ▲

At Bayside High, Screech stood nervously with Zack outside Mr. Belding's office.

"I don't know if I can walk through that door," Screech said, tugging at his collar.

"Hey, I've done it a million times," Zack reassured him. "Just don't trip over that little piece of loose carpeting near the bookcase."

"Do you really think he'll go for it?" Screech asked.

"Sure," Zack said. "He goes for everything. Well, almost. He didn't go for the free pizza delivery during assemblies. But even I admit that idea went a tad too far." Zack gave Screech a little push. "Come on, Screech. The bell just rang for homeroom. It's now or never. This is the only way out."

"Right," Screech said. "Just tell me again, Zack. Nobody at Bayside ever has to find out about this."

"Screech, nobody at Bayside ever has to find out about this," Zack said firmly. "Now—go."

Screech watched Zack head off toward homeroom. Then he straightened his shoulders and told himself to act like a man. He knocked on Mr. Belding's door.

"Come in!"

Screech pushed open the door. *Are you a man or a mouse, Screech?* he asked himself sternly.

Mr. Belding looked over his desk at him. "Yes, Samuel?"

"Eek," Screech said.

"Excuse me?"

"I mean, can I have a minute of your time, Mr. Belding?"

"Sure," Mr. Belding said. "Come on in."

Screech inched in. "It's about the senior class fund, Mr. Belding. I, uh, don't think I can deposit it today."

"Don't worry about it, Samuel," Mr. Belding said. "Deposit it later this week." Mr. Belding stared down again at the papers on his desk.

"Uh, Mr. Belding? I, uh, might not be able to deposit it then, either."

Mr. Belding looked up. He peered at Screech for a minute. "Why don't you shut the door and come on in, Screech," he said.

Screech closed the door and walked toward Mr. Belding. "You see, the thing is, I don't have the money," he said.

"You don't have the money," Mr. Belding repeated. "Then who does?"

Nervously, Screech perched on the ledge next to Mr. Belding's desk. He wiggled over and sat down next

to the PA system. "The class fund is gone, Mr. Belding,"
he said hesitantly. "And it's my fault."

▲   ▼   ▲

Mr. Loomis was in the middle of checking atten-
dance when the PA system suddenly switched on and
Screech's voice boomed out.

"The class fund is gone, Mr. Belding. And it's
my fault."

Zack sat up. *What was going on?* But, somehow,
he didn't even have to ask. Screech was a klutz under
the best of circumstances. Now, when he was nervous,
he had accidentally leaned on the ON button for the PA
system.

The whole class stared at the PA box as Mr.
Belding's voice came on. Even Mr. Loomis looked up.

"Gone?" Mr. Belding said. "What are you talking about?"

"I locked it in the drawer in the student council
room," Screech said. "But I guess somebody got to it."

"Screech, how could this have happened?" Mr.
Belding sounded upset.

"It happened because the guy's a dweeb, that's
why," Butch Henderson growled.

"Hey, can it, Butch," Slater said.

"Screech, this was your responsibility," Mr.
Belding said. "I picked you because I thought you were
trustworthy. Now the senior class is completely bank-

rupt. That means no Spring Frolic, and it will impact on the pep rally for the track team, too."

"Mr. Belding, I know that," Screech said. "And I feel awful about it. I—"

The sound cut off. Screech must have stopped leaning on the button.

The class sat silently for a moment. Then Daisy Tyler spoke up.

"No Spring Frolic!" she wailed.

"No pep rally!" Jeremy Frears said. He was a hurdler on the track team.

"That's what you get for giving the job to a dweeb," Butch said. "I say impeach him!"

"Impeach him!" Butch's buddy, Mac Zarillo, said.

The class took up the cry. Zack dropped his head in his hands. There was no way he could help Screech now. By second period, everyone would be blaming Screech. His friend was history.

Chapter 5

▲ ▼ ▲ ▼ ▲

The morning seemed to drag by for Kelly. Without Zack or Jessie or Lisa to walk with or giggle with in class, without Screech's outrageous comments and Slater's offer to carry her heavy load of books, school just wasn't the same. As a matter of fact, it was pretty boring. Kelly couldn't wait to get to the Max after school.

But she still had a major hurdle to get over before then: lunch.

Kelly paused at her locker while gray-skirted girls swirled around her. She heard chattering voices and laughter and teasing. She heard girls calling to each other to hurry up or to save a place at a table. She quickly got out the books she'd need for her afternoon classes. She'd just have to brave the cafeteria alone. She was starving.

She followed the stream of senior girls heading toward the double oak doors at the end of the hall. Then Kelly noticed that someone had swung into step next to her.

"Hi," the girl said. "You're the new girl, right?"

"Kelly Kapowski," Kelly said.

"I'm Ivy Templeton," the girl said. She had a clever face framed by short, curly dark hair. Her dark eyes didn't flick up and down Kelly as though she were inspecting her. They just looked at her in an interested way. "I hear the great white shark went into a feeding frenzy this morning."

"The great white shark?" Kelly asked, confused.

"Suki Ballard," Ivy said in a low voice. She glanced around her quickly. "Keep your voice down; she has spies everywhere."

Kelly laughed, but then she realized that Ivy was serious. "You make her sound scary."

"She is," Ivy said flatly. "Look, I think of this school as a shark tank. That's why I call Suki a great white. She's the scariest man-eater of them all."

"I think Suki thought I was making fun of her, but I really wasn't," Kelly said. "Maybe I should apologize."

"Wouldn't do any good," Ivy said. "Actually, it would make things worse. She'd think you were weak. Then she'd eat you for breakfast."

"What are you saying, Ivy?" Kelly asked her in a low tone as they pushed open the doors of the cafeteria. "I've gotten on Suki Ballard's bad side so I might as well forget it?"

"You learn fast, kid," Ivy said. "Look, you may have thought that Miss Rumson runs the school. *Wrong.* Suki does."

Suddenly, Kelly stopped in astonishment as she noticed the cafeteria. It was a long, oak-paneled room with soft carpets. Round oak tables in various sizes were scattered about, and real china with linen napkins were at each chair. Waitresses in black uniforms were already placing plates of food in front of early arrivals. And instead of the bustle and noise of Bayside, conversation was hushed.

"Wow," Kelly said. "This is the cafeteria? It looks like a restaurant."

"It's the dining hall," Ivy corrected. "Don't *ever* call it the cafeteria. Come on, there's a table for two by the window."

Gratefully, Kelly settled into a chair by a lace-curtained window. Sunlight made a pool of warmth on the table and chased away some of the dark, gloomy feeling of the paneled room.

Ivy shook out her napkin and placed it on her lap. "Even lunch is part of the curriculum," she said to Kelly. "Teachers walk around correcting your table manners, so be careful. The waitress will give you a choice of some kind of meat or chicken dish or soup and salad. Get the soup and salad. It's the lesser of two evils."

Kelly laughed. "I hope it's better than the food at Bayside."

"Don't count on it," Ivy said sourly. "Just because our parents pay about a trillion dollars to send us here doesn't mean the food's any better than at public school."

"Tell me about Suki," Kelly said, sipping at a glass of ice water. "Why does everyone listen to her except you?"

"Whoa, don't get the wrong idea, Kelly," Ivy said. "I'm the same weasel everybody else is. I don't have any courage. I'm barely hanging on here by my fingernails, and you can see what shape *they're* in." She held up a handful of bitten nails for Kelly's inspection.

"What do you mean, you're barely hanging on?" Kelly asked.

Ivy sighed. "My father is unemployed at the moment. He ran a savings and loan. So he'll either get indicted, in which case I'm out on my ear, or he'll need a new job. He says I have to make *connections* for him here. And Suki's father is a major honcho in L.A."

"Gosh," Kelly said. "Things certainly are complicated here."

"You said it," Ivy said gloomily.

The waitress came by, and Kelly and Ivy ordered the potato-leek soup and crabmeat salad.

"What does your father do, Kelly?" Ivy asked.

"He's the foreman at a plant in Bayside," Kelly said. "Consolidated Technologies."

"He's a *foreman*? Really? Wow," Ivy said, as though Kelly had just said her dad was a big game hunter or an astronaut. "That's incredible."

Just then, a shadow darkened the sunny table. Kelly looked up and saw Suki.

"Hi, Suki," Kelly said. She refused to let the girl intimidate her. "Listen, I'm sorry we got off on the wrong foot this morning. I didn't mean to—"

"I don't know what you're talking about, Kapowski," Suki said smoothly. She turned to Ivy. "Hi, Templeton. That's a cute cardigan."

"Thanks, Suki," Ivy said quickly. "It's my favorite."

Suki turned to Kelly. "And those are darling pearls, Kapowski."

Kelly reached for the unfamiliar necklace and fingered it. "Thanks. My aunt gave them to me."

"Oh?" Suki said with acid sweetness. "Hey, I just realized what they remind me of. Something someone would wear on one of those old sitcoms on cable. And a charm bracelet, too? Oooo, how...*retro*. Is your aunt's name Donna Reed?"

Before her remark even registered, Suki had turned to Ivy. "Listen, Templeton. Heather, Shannon, Michelle, and I want you to come sit at our table. You're really good in history, and we are like totally lost."

"S-sit at *your* table?" Ivy stammered.

"That's correct, Templeton. Think you can handle it?"

Ivy looked down at her lap. She looked at the window. She looked everywhere but at Kelly. "Sure," she said finally.

Suki's silver bracelets clanked as she flipped her blond hair over her shoulder. "Have a good lunch, Kapowski," she said.

Kelly didn't say anything. Ivy shot her a guilty look and followed Suki across the thick carpet. Conversation in the room lowered as everyone noticed Kelly sitting alone. At Suki's table, a foursome of very pretty girls all glanced at Kelly, then back at each other. They laughed.

The waitress placed a steaming bowl of potato-leek soup in front of Kelly. No matter what Ivy had said, it smelled delicious. Kelly picked up her spoon. But suddenly, she wasn't hungry anymore.

▲   ▼   ▲

By the afternoon, the IMPEACH SCREECH! campaign was in full swing. As fast as Mr. Belding ordered the posters torn down, new ones went up again. Even though Screech knew that his friends were on his side, it was still hard to walk around school with everyone giving him dirty looks. Screech made a special trip to his locker for his sunglasses. But he still felt exposed when he walked around the halls. Besides, he kept bumping into things.

Finally, the last bell rang, and Screech hurried toward the school exit. On his way, he passed Mr. Belding at the window overlooking the parking lot.

"Mr. Belding?" Screech approached him cautiously. Mr. Belding had been pretty great about everything, but Screech wasn't exactly his favorite person at the moment. "I just wanted to thank you again for not firing me yet," Screech said.

But Mr. Belding didn't look as though he heard him. His forehead suddenly hit the glass with a clunk. "Not my Miata!" he moaned.

"What is it, Mr. B?" Screech asked, coming to the window and looking out. He saw Mr. Belding's red Miata being driven out of the parking lot. "Is someone stealing your car?" he yelped. "Maybe it's the thief!"

"No, Screech," Mr. Belding said, turning away from the window. "It's being repossessed. Mrs. Belding has forgotten to make my car payments to the leasing company for four months."

"Gosh, Mr. Belding," Screech said. "It sounds like Mrs. Belding and I are in the same boat."

"Yeah, and it's sinking fast," Mr. Belding said.

"What about Pete?" Screech asked sympathetically. Old Pete was probably Mr. Belding's grandfather or great-uncle. Screech hated to think of some old guy needing an operation and not getting it.

"Oh, I solved that problem at least," Mr. Belding said with a sigh. "I'm going to check him into the hospital tomorrow."

"Well, give him my best," Screech said. He saw Zack heading down the hall, and he hurried toward him.

"Come on, Screech, let's hit the Max," Zack said. "We've got plans to make, and I can't think if I'm dehydrated."

Phyllis Ptowski walked up to them. She was wearing a short skirt and cowboy boots, and she looked great. "Are you guys heading for the Max? Can I walk over with you?"

"Sure, Phyllis," Zack said uneasily. He hoped that Kelly wouldn't already be there.

But Kelly was sitting with Slater, Jessie, and Lisa when he walked through the door. When she saw Phyllis with him, she frowned.

"Hi, Kelly!" Zack said cheerfully. "Excuse me, Phyllis. Catch you later." He hurried over to Kelly and gave her a kiss.

"Hi," Kelly said coolly.

"Phyllis asked if she could walk with us," Zack said.

"It's true," Screech said.

Kelly sighed. "You could have said no."

"Kelly, I don't want to hurt her feelings," Zack protested.

"I know," Kelly said. "But I don't think you're being clear enough. She's always *around*, Zack. Are you sure you're not giving her any encouragement?"

"Not at all," Zack said. It was true. He'd been nice to Phyllis, but he never flirted with her. But it was time to change the subject. "Tell us about your first day, Kelly. What was Miss Fopp's like?"

Zack's voice carried, and a few kids drifted closer to listen.

"Well...it's a gorgeous school," Kelly said. "It has all these oil paintings and these thick carpets. And they have about twice as many computers as Bayside for half as many students. You should see the parking lot, Zack. It's full of Porsches and Mercedes. And one Ferrari. And the cafeteria is called a dining hall, and it looks like a restaurant. It has tablecloths and real plates and real napkins." Kelly found herself talking a lot about the school itself because she didn't want to talk about the people.

"Wow," Lisa breathed. "It sounds fantastic."

"I bet you don't miss Bayside," Tamara Talbot said enviously, moving closer.

"She'd be crazy if she did," Eloise Myers said.

"I guess," Kelly said weakly. "So what happened at Bayside today?"

"Oh, you don't want to hear about that, Kelly," Lisa said.

"It's pretty boring compared to Miss Fopp's," Jessie added.

"No, really," Kelly said. "What did Ms. Meadows make for lunch today?"

"Ugh," Tamara said. "This awful vegetarian casserole."

"A total gross-out feast," Slater said.

"What did they serve at Miss Fopp's, Kelly?" Eloise asked.

"This delicious potato-leek soup, and a crab-meat salad," Kelly said. "The waitress was really—"

"Waitress?" Tamara said. "You have *waitresses* at school?"

"Well, yes," Kelly said. Suddenly, she felt uncomfortable talking about Miss Fopp's. Tamara and Eloise were looking at her in a strange way. They exchanged a glance.

"We'd better get back to our table," Tamara said.

After they left, Kelly turned to the gang. "So how is the investigation going?"

"That reminds me," Zack said. "I thought of our first step."

Screech whipped out a pad and pencil. "I'm ready, chief."

"Access," Zack said. "That's the key, so to speak. Who else had a key to the student council room?"

"All the members of the student council," Jessie said, shrugging.

"And what about the drawer?"

"Just me," Screech said.

"So you *think*," Zack said. "How do we know that Babette never made a key for someone else? We should ask her, at least."

"Of course!" Screech exclaimed. "I'll call her right now. I have her number. Come on, Zack."

He rushed over to the pay phone. Zack followed more slowly. Flipping open his notebook to read the number, Screech punched out Babette's phone number. Screech's hopes rose when she answered the phone.

"Babette? Hi, it's Screech. How are you?"

Babette coughed weakly into the phone. "Not too good. My throat's real sore and I'm totally weak. I feel like a wet washcloth."

"Oh, that's too bad," Screech said. "What does the doctor say?"

Zack rolled his eyes as Screech kept nodding and saying "Uh-huh" into the phone. Babette was known as a big talker. She could go on for hours. Zack waited, but when Screech asked Babette if she'd rented any good videos, Zack lost patience. He grabbed the phone away.

"Hi, Babette, it's Zack," he said. "I'm sorry you're not feeling well."

"Thanks," Babette said. "My head aches and I'm real tired."

"That's great," Zack said. "Listen, I guess you heard that the senior class fund was stolen."

"Yeah," Babette said. "Bummer. It's almost as bad as having mono. Did I mention I have a fever?"

"That's nice," Zack said. "Babette, we're trying to catch the thief, and we were wondering if you ever made a copy of the key to that drawer."

"No, I'd never do that," Babette said. "I kept it on me all the time. The key chain snapped right into my purse, so it was always safe. I never let my purse out of my sight."

"Oh," Zack said, disappointed. "Well, thanks, anyway. I hope you feel bett—"

"I was always real careful about my purse," Babette said. "That's why I was so upset when I thought I lost it that time."

Zack gripped the phone. "You lost your purse?"

"Well, only for about a half hour, tops," Babette said. "I misplaced it. But it was really there all the time." She coughed into the receiver, and Zack hoped mono germs didn't fly over phone lines.

"Babette, what are you talking about?" Zack asked patiently.

"It was during the Valley High football game the

Saturday before last. I put it down by my feet on the bleachers while I watched the game. When I went to get a tissue, like ten minutes later—it was still the first quarter, I remember, because A. C. Slater didn't have mud on his little tight pants yet—hey, aren't you best friends with Slater? He's so cute."

Zack closed his eyes. "Babette. Your purse."

"Oh, right. I reached for a tissue—you see, I was already sick then, but I thought it was just a cold—and it wasn't there. My friend Camille and I looked everywhere. Finally, I thought maybe I left it in the little girls' room so we checked in there. It wasn't there, but I *did* get a tissue and blow my nose. Then, when we got back to the bleachers, we saw it underneath my scarf. It must have been there all along. Silly, huh? I was really freaked out for about fifteen minutes."

"Well, at least you got it back," Zack said absently. He was thinking hard.

Babette blew her nose into the receiver. "Anyway, two days later, my mom took me to the doctor and we found out I had mono. I have to stay in bed for at least two weeks. I feel just awful."

"That's nice," Zack said. "Take care, Babette. Thanks a lot." He hung up the receiver and turned to Screech. "I know how the thief got into the drawer!" he exclaimed.

"You do?" Screech brightened.

"All we have to do is follow the trail," Zack said, clapping Screech on the back. "Then we'll catch him red-handed."

"Gosh, was he wearing gloves?" Screech said. "I

guess that's because he didn't want to leave fingerprints. But how do you know they were red?"

Zack closed his eyes for a moment to gather his patience. "Come on, Screech," he said. "Let's tell the others."

They went back to the table and told the gang the good news. Zack explained what they had to do.

"So when do we get started?" Kelly asked.

"Kelly, you don't have to worry about it," Zack said. "We'll have to leave right from Bayside tomorrow. We'll meet you here later."

"Oh," Kelly said.

"So tomorrow morning, we'll make out a list," Zack said to the gang. "We can meet at our lockers before homeroom."

Everyone nodded in agreement. Kelly took a sip of her soda. She'd only been gone for one day. But already she felt like she wasn't part of Bayside anymore.

Chapter 6

▲ ▼ ▲ ▼ ▲

That night, Kelly knocked on her parents' bedroom door. When she heard her mother call "Come in," she pushed it open. Her mother was in bed, reading, and her father was sitting in the armchair with headphones on, listening to music.

"What is it, sweetie?" her mother asked. She looked over the top of her book at Kelly and smiled. Mrs. Kapowski had Kelly's same deep blue eyes, but her dark hair was cut in a short, feathery style.

Her father took off his earphones. "What's up, pumpkin?"

Kelly sighed. "I'm having a bad week."

Her mother laughed. "It's only Monday." But when Kelly only gave a weak smile, her mother said gently, "I thought you were awfully quiet at dinner. Don't you like Miss Fopp's at all?"

"Well," Kelly said cautiously, "so far, it hasn't been one of my favorite experiences." It was hard to tell her parents how completely and utterly she loathed Miss Fopp's. They were really hoping that she would like it.

"It's always hard to go to a new school," her mother said.

"Especially when the school is full of snobs," Kelly said. "I hate it!"

Her mother patted her knee. "I'm sure there are nice girls there, too. You'll make friends."

"I don't think so," Kelly mumbled. "With friends like them, who needs enemies?"

"Just be yourself, and everyone will love you," her mother continued.

"Just give them a chance," Mr. Kapowski said. "Kelly, you're the smartest and prettiest girl there, I bet. Maybe some of the girls are jealous. But the ones who are genuinely nice will come around."

Kelly looked at her dear, wonderful parents. They were so lame sometimes. They thought that everyone would be crazy about her just because they were. They were confusing high school with a normal existence. They didn't know that high school was a wild, savage jungle filled with snake pits. Or a shark tank, Kelly thought, remembering what Ivy had said.

"I know it must be hard," her mother said. "But you've only been there for one day, honey. Give it a chance."

I could give it twenty years, and I'd still want to blow the place up! Kelly wanted to say. But she didn't. Parents didn't understand that stuff.

"I feel so out of place there," she tried. "I stick out like a sore thumb because I'm wearing regular clothes. Everybody is always looking me up and down."

"That reminds me!" her mother said. "Your uniform is ready. It hardly needed any alterations, so it will be at school waiting for you tomorrow. Isn't that great?"

"Great," Kelly said halfheartedly. Now, not only would she be miserable, she'd be dressed like a geek.

Her father got up from his chair and came over to sit next to her. "I know it must be tough to leave all your friends," he said. "But you don't have too much longer to go in your senior year. And now, since Mrs. Lenihan is helping you, we can help Nicki and the others more."

Kelly felt her heart fall. It was true. If she turned down Marion's money, it would make it tougher on her brothers and sisters. Now there would be more money for them. How selfish could she be?

Kelly summoned up a smile. "You're right," she said to her parents. "I just need to give it some time." She kissed them both good night and went back to her room. She was stuck at Miss Fopp's. There was no turning back.

▲   ▼   ▲

On Tuesday morning, Zack met everyone at their lockers.

"Let's go over this again," he said. "Someone took Babette's purse, stole the key, and made a copy.

Then they ran back to the gym and returned the bag while Babette was in the bathroom. Babette swears that it was only about fifteen minutes from when she noticed it was missing until she found it again. Allowing ten extra minutes while she was watching the game, I figure that gives someone about half an hour to make a duplicate key and come back. So I looked up all the places you could get keys made within fifteen minutes of Bayside."

He held up a piece of paper. "Here they are."

"Okay," Jessie said. "Let's divide it up."

"Wait a second," Slater said. "What if Babette was right and her purse wasn't really missing? After all, she said she found it underneath her scarf."

"I'm betting that the thief put it back and then covered it with the scarf so she'd think she'd been mistaken," Zack said.

"Well, what else do we have to go on?" Lisa said. "We don't have any other leads."

"The only hitch is that Babette didn't have the key to the student council room in her purse," Zack said. "It was in her locker."

"That actually helps us narrow it down," Jessie said. "Maybe whoever took the key has their own key to the council room."

"We'll have to find that out next," Zack said. "Okay, here's the list. There's ten places the person might have gone, and there's five of us. So each of us will take two places and ask if the storekeeper can remember making a key the Saturday before last."

"This seems kind of hopeless," Lisa said. "They must make a million keys."

"Not really," Zack said. "We're not in a major shopping district. It would be different if we had to ask at the mall, or over on Spruce Road, where everybody shops. We might luck out. And if you ask if the person was in a big hurry, that might help." He shrugged. "I think it's worth a shot for Screech's sake, don't you?"

"*I* think it's worth it for my sake," Screech said fervently.

Lisa smiled. "So do we, Screech."

"Here we go," Zack said. He ripped the list into five pieces and gave each person the addresses of two stores to try. "First thing after school, we head out to catch a thief."

▲   ▼   ▲

The gang still hadn't reached the Max when Kelly arrived that afternoon. She stood uneasily in the doorway in her gray uniform. Everyone turned around and stared. It was almost as bad as being at Miss Fopp's. She'd had to eat lunch alone again today. Ivy Templeton had whispered to her that Suki Ballard had passed the word that the new girl was to be kept in an isolation ward. Then Ivy had scurried away.

Kelly went down the stairs and headed for her usual table. At least she was used to eating alone now. She'd never eaten alone in public in her life until she'd transferred out of Bayside. On the way, she passed Tamara and Eloise, who were sitting with Daisy Tyler and a couple of the cheerleaders.

"Hey," Tamara said, eyeing Kelly's knee-length gray skirt. "I didn't realize the Max had a dress code."

Kelly blushed. "It's my new uniform," she said. "Everyone at Miss Fopp's has to wear one." She dabbed at her blouse. "I already spilled raspberry jam on it during deportment class."

"Deportment class? What's that?" Eloise asked.

"It's like etiquette, only more complicated," Kelly explained. "Today we learned how to give a tea party."

"Well, la-di-da," Daisy Tyler said, rolling her baby blue eyes.

"I guess that could come in handy someday," Jean-Marie Howell said doubtfully.

"It sounds snobby to me," Eloise said.

"Well," Kelly said faintly, "I guess I should go to my table."

"See you," Tamara said.

Kelly started to slide into the booth, but suddenly, she couldn't. She couldn't sit here alone, waiting for everyone to show up. She had had enough of feeling conspicuous at Miss Fopp's. She turned on her heel and walked out of the Max.

Tamara Talbot watched her go. "I guess the waitresses here aren't as good as at Miss Fopp's," she said. "Kelly just couldn't wait."

"She's gotten really snobby," Eloise said. "Yesterday, you should have heard her bragging about the dining hall. I mean, excuse me. A cafeteria is just fine by me."

Daisy took a sip of soda. "It *did* seem like she was trying to impress us," she said.

"How to give a tea party? I mean, really," Jean-Marie agreed. "I guess *Countess* Kelly has really changed since she went to Miss Fopp's."

The girls all nodded. "Well, we shouldn't tell anyone what a snob Kelly is now," Tamara said. "It might be just a phase or something."

"True," Eloise said. "You're right, Tamara. Personally, my lips are absolutely sealed."

▲　　▼　　▲

When the gang straggled into the Max a half hour later, it was practically deserted. Zack was the last to arrive. He slid into the booth next to Jessie.

"Any luck?" he asked. But he could tell by their faces that nobody had a lead. Everyone shook their heads.

"Either they didn't remember, or it was too busy that day," Jessie said with a sigh.

"I thought I came close," Slater said. "This guy started to describe someone, a teenage guy, who wanted a key in a hurry. But then he remembered that it was just this *last* Saturday."

"I waited around for one of the workers at Ed's Hardware," Zack said. "He was on his coffee break. When he came in, he said he'd made a bunch of keys the

Saturday before last. But he couldn't remember who he'd cut them for."

Screech dropped his head in his hands. "I'm finished," he wailed. "Impeached during my first term in office!"

"Don't give up yet, Screech," Jessie said. "We'll think of something. I hope."

"Maybe nobody made a key at all," Lisa said, frowning. "Some people are really good at picking locks. Once when I locked myself out of the house, Tony Berlando opened my door with a credit card. He told me he got really good at it because he's always misplacing his house keys."

"Tony Berlando?" Zack asked, sitting up. "Didn't he just buy a mountain bike? And at the dance, he told me that he was bummed that he couldn't bid on a surfing lesson with his girlfriend because he didn't have any money."

"That's right," Jessie said. "And that girlfriend happens to be Melissa Alden. She's on the student council."

"And he's on the wrestling team," Slater said. "We had a meet on Saturday at Bayside."

"That's when I figure the money was stolen," Screech said. "Plenty of people were at school for clubs and sports, but no council members. Nobody would see someone break into the student council room."

Zack snapped his fingers. "Motive, method, and opportunity," he said triumphantly. "Maybe we've found our man!"

Chapter 7

▲ ▼ ▲ ▼ ▲

Kelly called Zack that night, but he was busy working on Screech's case, and they hung up after only five minutes. She tossed and turned all night, dreading the next day at school. The next morning, she had a stomachache. But she got on the bus and went to school.

Kelly walked down the hall toward deportment class. Her main nightmare last night had involved Ms. Letitia Tolan, the deportment teacher. She'd been standing over her, yelling at her as Kelly poured hot tea on her very own foot.

Yesterday's tea-party class had been a nightmare all on its own. It had started with a lesson on how to make tea. Kelly had thought that she already *knew* how to make tea. You slosh a tea bag around in some hot water, then add a splash of milk from the carton and a little squirt of honey from a plastic bear, and you're in

Beverage City. So when Ms. Tolan had called her over, Kelly had asked where the tea bag was. Everyone had burst out laughing.

There turned out to be much more involved in making tea than Kelly had imagined. First of all, you didn't use a tea bag at all. You used loose tea and dumped it in a porcelain teapot. Then there were strainers and cozies and silver tongs for sugar and the right way to pour and when to hand out the napkins. Kelly spent the whole class knowing that she'd never use this stuff. If she had friends over, she'd just do what she always did—pass out Diet Cokes and potato chips.

Kelly walked cautiously into the room. Deportment class was more informal than history or chemistry or English. They met in the library of the school, a place with a huge Oriental rug, overstuffed couches, armchairs, and a fireplace. It was the most beautiful room Kelly had ever been in, but she couldn't relax enough to enjoy it.

First of all, the girls tended to sit with their friends. They would drag chairs together or sit next to each other on the couches. Everyone always left the deep red velvet couch free for Suki Ballard and her friends. No matter how late Suki got to class, the most comfortable couch sat empty and waiting for her.

Before Kelly had taken a small chintz armchair in the corner. But someone was already sitting in it today. Kelly looked quickly around. Next to her, Ursula LaPoint was looking, too. Ursula was a tall, intelligent girl in Kelly's English class.

"Looks like the love seat is still empty," she said to Kelly. "Let's grab it."

Finally! Kelly thought. *Someone is being friendly to me.* But as she and Ursula threaded through the chairs and tables toward the small sofa in the rear, Kelly heard Suki's voice. "Ursula! Over here!"

Suki patted the seat next to her on the big, red velvet couch. Ursula blushed, looking pleased.

"I'll catch you later, Kelly," she said.

"Sure," Kelly said, but Ursula was already gone, hurrying over to sit next to Suki.

Kelly sank down on the love seat. This just kept happening to her. All the girls were in different cliques, and hardly anyone ever made an effort to befriend her. But whenever somebody did, somehow Suki Ballard managed to spoil it!

Ms. Tolan entered, and the girls quieted immediately. She announced that today's class would involve the proper way to pay a social call. Somehow, Kelly had a feeling this would not involve standing on the lawn and bellowing, "Hey, Jessie! Get the lead out! I'm waiting!"

Kelly tried to concentrate while Ms. Tolan explained that just because the custom had become less practiced in today's world didn't mean that a lady shouldn't know how to conduct herself.

"Remember, ladies," Ms. Tolan said, "during your posture class in the beginning of the term, how everyone had groaned and said they already knew how to walk? Well, the posture training came in handy, didn't it?"

Everyone in the class nodded agreement. Kelly hadn't taken the class, but she nodded, anyway, just to be polite. Ms. Tolan was a severe, disciplined woman who demanded obedience.

Ms. Tolan shot them a sly look. "I'm glad you agree with me, girls," she said. "Because today you just might be called upon to demonstrate that, as Fopp girls, you have impeccable posture and carriage."

"What is it, Ms. Tolan?" one of the girls asked.

"The charity luncheon at the Beverly Grande Hotel," Ms. Tolan said. "There will be a special role for a few Miss Fopp's ladies there this year."

A murmur of excitement went through the class. Kelly raised her hand. "Ms. Tolan? What charity does the luncheon benefit?"

Ms. Tolan looked confused. "Well, actually, Miss Kapowski, I'm not quite certain. Does anyone know?"

All the girls exchanged glances and shrugged.

"How about you, Miss Ballard? Do you know?" Ms. Tolan asked. She turned to the class. "This year, Mrs. Wendell Ballard is the chairperson of the event."

Suki flipped her hair over one shoulder. "I'm not sure, Ms. Tolan. I'll ask Mother. But I'm sure it's a totally *crucial* charity."

"Mrs. Ballard has instituted an innovation this year," Ms. Tolan said excitedly. "Now, as we're all aware, the luncheon involves a fashion show, each year with a different designer. And the models every year are, of course, society women. Some of your very own mothers have participated in the past. But this year, Mrs. Ballard has decreed that striding down that runway along with the wives of the most socially prominent men in the Los Angeles area will be the *daughters.*" Ms. Tolan spread her hands. "You."

Everyone began to talk at once. "Mother told me last night," Suki said in a loud voice. "I think it's a fabulous idea."

"Unfortunately, there are several schools in the Los Angeles area that will be participating," Ms. Tolan said with a sniff. "Of course, Miss Fopp's is the best of them, but we must be fair. There will only be three girls chosen from each school."

"Suki, you're in for sure," Suki's best friend, Heather, whispered.

"Everyone has an equal chance," Ms. Tolan said. "Melvin Fine himself will be visiting after school today to *personally* choose the three girls."

"Melvin Fine!" someone squealed. "His clothes are gorgeous!"

"I'm definitely trying out," someone else said.

Kelly sighed. Normally, she'd be right there with the rest of the girls, hoping to be chosen. She'd even been in a fashion show before. But without any friends to do it with, the show just wouldn't be fun.

After school, Kelly decided to head straight to the Max. There was no way she was going to stay at Miss Fopp's for one second longer than she had to.

▲   ▼   ▲

Jessie ran into the cafeteria at lunch and came straight to the gang's table. "Okay," she said in a low voice. "I've spotted our man. He's in the music room."

Zack put down his half-eaten sandwich. "Let's go."

All day, they'd been waiting for the perfect time to talk to Tony Berlando. He hadn't been outside school this morning, and when he hadn't shown up at the cafeteria, they'd thought they were out of luck. Jessie had volunteered for reconnaissance work and had roamed the halls looking for him.

When they got close to the music room, Zack held up a hand, and they stopped.

"Okay, gang," he said in a low voice. "Remember what we talked about. We have to play him like a fish. Offer the bait. Tantalize. Sympathize. Only then do we try to reel him in. Don't be obvious. Subtle is the way to go."

"Subtle," Screech repeated, nodding.

"Okay," Zack said. "Let's go."

They pushed open the door to the music room, where Tony was practicing his saxophone. He stopped when he saw them come in.

"Tony, it's you," Zack said. "We heard this dynamite music, and we had to see who was playing."

"We thought it was a tape," Jessie said. "I didn't know you played the saxophone."

Tony nodded modestly. "Yeah, since I was a kid."

"It sounded fantastic," Lisa said.

Tony blushed at the attention. It was hard to imagine him as a cold-blooded thief, Zack thought. Somehow, you didn't think a thief would be *shy*.

"Screech should have hired you to play with the band at the dance last Friday," Lisa said.

Jessie moved closer and sat down next to Tony. "Were you at the dance? I didn't see you."

Tony nodded. "I went with Melissa Alden."

"I know Melissa," Jessie said. "I'm on the student council with her."

"Speaking of the student council," Zack said, "isn't it awful that someone stole the senior class fund?"

"You said it," Tony said, nodding. "I can't imagine why someone would do something like that."

"It *is* hard to imagine," Slater said. "But we've all been tempted by something once in our lives. Sometimes, it's hard to resist, I guess."

"It doesn't mean the thief is necessarily a bad person," Lisa said.

"They might even regret what they did, and want to give back the money," Jessie said.

"If you say so," Tony said, fingering his sax. "But maybe they're enjoying the money and are glad that they didn't get caught."

The gang exchanged glances. Could Tony be playing a cat-and-mouse game with them?

"I noticed your new bike this morning, Tony," Zack said offhandedly. "It's totally cool."

"Thanks," Tony said. "I've been wanting it for a while. I ride about five miles to school every day, and it was a drag riding my old bike. The chain kept falling off on the hills."

"I could see where you'd want a new bike," Lisa said.

"It must have been hard to walk up all those hills," Jessie said, her hazel eyes soft with sympathy.

Tony seemed to melt toward her. "It's nice of you to sympathize," he said, gazing into Jessie's eyes.

Perfect, Zack thought. *Everyone was following through. They were reeling him in, and he didn't even know it.*

Then, Screech whipped out a memo pad. "All right, Berlando, where were you on the afternoon of the twenty-sixth?"

Tony sat up, startled by Screech's crisp tone. "Huh?"

"We've got your number, bub," Screech said.

"Screech," Zack said fiercely. "Shut up!"

"Oh, that's right," Screech said. "I should read him his rights first. Okay, Berlando. You have the right to remain silent, but if you do, Slater will hang you out the window by your ankles."

Tony stood up. "Hey, what's going on here?" he asked. He looked from one face to another. "Whoa, wait a second. Do you guys think that *I* stole the money?"

Everyone shuffled their feet nervously. "Well...," Zack said.

"Thanks a lot," Tony said. He looked really

upset. "You guys come in here and flatter my saxophone playing, and all that time, you were just trying to nail me to the wall for something I didn't do."

"Tony, help us out here," Zack said. "If you're innocent, you won't mind telling us how you got the money to pay for that bike."

"I got the bike for my birthday on Sunday, not that it's any of your business," Tony said.

"Were you at school last Saturday?" Jessie asked.

Tony nodded. "For a wrestling meet. Slater saw me."

"Sure," Slater said. "But I wasn't with you every second. I didn't see you after the meet was over."

"But Mike Meridian did," Tony said. "We showered and then left together for a burger at the Max."

"And Sunday?" Screech asked.

"Sunday was my birthday. My parents had a party, and Melissa was there. I also took her to the movies Saturday night. As a matter of fact, I was with somebody or other practically every second all weekend. So I have an alibi, okay?"

"Tony, we're really sorry," Lisa said. "But we really want to get to the bottom of this."

Tony began to pack away his sax. "If you want to get to the bottom of it, why don't you use your brains?" he asked bitterly. "I can think of at least one person who would benefit from having that money stolen."

"Who?" Zack asked.

Tony turned around. "Babette was totally

freaked about giving up her position as class treasurer. Melissa told me that she's afraid that when she *does* come back, no one will want her to be treasurer anymore. She wasn't very good at it, you know. It was her fault we were almost bankrupt in the first place."

"So she'd *want* Screech to fail," Zack said slowly.

"And she's not totally bedridden, so she could have come to school on Saturday and taken the money," Jessie said, thinking. "She knew that Screech would have to lock it up over the weekend."

Tony snapped his sax case shut. "So would you mind leaving me out of this? I'm totally innocent."

Jessie touched his arm. "Tony, we really *are* sorry. But Screech is our best friend. We're just trying to help him out. Can you understand that?"

Tony nodded reluctantly. "I guess so. But I just want you guys to tell me one thing."

"Sure," Zack said. "You name it."

"Did you *really* mean it when you said you thought I was a great sax player?"

"We really meant it," the gang chorused. They definitely owed Tony. But behind their backs, Jessie, Slater, Screech, Zack, and Lisa all had their fingers well crossed.

▲   ▼   ▲

Kelly grabbed her blazer from her locker and hurried down the hall. She couldn't wait to get into the fresh air. Even though it was embarrassing to have to wait for the bus while the rest of the girls drove off in their expensive cars, she was ecstatic to be out of the Fopp atmosphere.

She had almost reached the front door when Ms. Tolan emerged from the library. "Miss Kapowski!" she said. "Where are you going? Mr. Fine is already here and the rest of the girls have gathered in the dining hall."

"I wasn't planning to try out, Ms. Tolan," Kelly said.

"What? Don't be ridiculous. You're a lovely girl, and your carriage is excellent, even though you missed that class," Ms. Tolan fussed. "Miss Kapowski, you're new here, so you should enter into the spirit of Miss Fopp's wholeheartedly. Now come along with me."

What could Kelly do? Kelly had never said no to a teacher, and she wasn't about to start with Ms. Tolan. She allowed Ms. Tolan to lead her down the hall toward the dining hall.

Kelly bit her lip nervously. She had wanted to avoid trying out for this at all costs. It would put her in competition with Suki Ballard. Was she making a major mistake?

Chapter 8

▲ ▼ ▲ ▼ ▲

The chairs and tables in the dining hall had been pushed to the side so that an aisle ran straight down the middle of the room. Kelly recognized the famous designer Melvin Fine at the end of the aisle, sitting in a carved walnut chair. He was watching one of the girls from Miss Fopp's walk down the aisle, and Kelly realized that the aisle was supposed to be a fashion show runway. The auditions had already begun.

Ms. Tolan pushed her to the end of the line where the other girls were waiting. Kelly found herself staring at the back of Suki's blond head. *Great,* Kelly groaned inwardly. No matter how she tried to stay out of Suki's way, she always ended up thrown right in the shark tank with her.

Suki was talking in a loud voice to her friends Heather and Michelle. Kelly realized that Suki never lowered her voice when she had a conversation. She just didn't care if anyone was listening or not. She probably figured everyone at Miss Fopp's was wildly interested in whatever she had to say.

"He's major adorable," Suki was saying. "But also *dangerous*. Like James Dean."

"Oooo," Michelle said breathlessly. Then she hesitated. "Who's James Dean?"

Suki gave her a cold look. "Get a life, Pierce. He's only the sexiest actor *ever.*"

"What have I seen him in lately?" Michelle asked, frowning.

"He's dead, Michelle," Heather said. "Give it a rest, will you? So, Suki, what kind of car does this guy drive?"

"That's the best part," Suki said. "He doesn't drive a car. He has this wicked Harley."

"I thought your mother wouldn't let you ride on a motorcycle," Michelle said.

Suki tossed her head. "So?" Her lips curved in a catlike smile. "What the warden doesn't know won't hurt her, right?"

"You mean your parents have never met him?" Michelle asked. "Wow. My parents won't even let me *breathe* on a guy if they don't know his family."

"I told Mom she could meet him at the charity luncheon," Suki said. "He's going to pick me up. On his motorcycle. I can't wait to see her face!"

"If I wasn't a complete and utter *cynic*, I'd say this was true love," Heather said.

Suki shrugged. "Who knows? He has everything—looks, danger, money. He's the most exciting boy I've ever met. No, wait a second. Did I say *boy*? Denny is a man."

Kelly's ears pricked up. Denny? That wasn't a very common name. Could Suki be talking about Denny Vane? He rode a Harley and he certainly looked dangerous. But Kelly had known Denny since kindergarten, so she knew he was really a nice guy whose worst crime was cheating at Trivial Pursuit.

Still, it was impossible to imagine Suki Ballard ever hooking up with someone like Denny Vane. Denny was definitely from the wrong side of the tracks.

"Look," Suki said, holding out her arm. "He gave me this last night." She turned her arm from side to side to show off a new watch.

"Is that gold?" Michelle asked. "I hope so."

"Of *course* it's gold," Suki said. "Which is kind of a drag, since my signature look is based around silver. But I think it was sweet of Denny, anyway. Maybe he'll get me some gold bracelets to go with it."

"Watch out, Michelle," Heather said. "It looks like Suki might win the bet and get married first. Soon we'll be having teas with Mrs. Denny Vane."

Kelly couldn't believe it. Suki's boyfriend *was* Denny Vane! The thought of Suki pouring out tea in the ramshackle Vane house while Denny lounged in black leather made her laugh out loud.

Suki turned around and gave her a frosty gaze. "What's so funny, Kapowski?"

"Well, I *know* Denny," Kelly said. "He goes to my old school."

"You mean he doesn't go to private school?" Heather asked.

"It must be a different Denny," Suki said quickly.

"No, really," Kelly said. "He—"

"What are you *doing* here, anyway, Kapowski?" Suki asked. "Don't tell me you're trying out?"

Kelly lifted her chin. "Yes, I am."

Suki's gaze flicked over Kelly, and one corner of her mouth lifted. "Well, good luck," she said. Then she turned her back on Kelly again. "She'll need it," she said to Heather and Michelle in a voice she surely wanted Kelly to overhear.

"Hey, I'm next," Michelle said. "I'm so nervous!"

"Don't worry, Michelle. He's not going to pick you," Suki said. "You're too short."

Michelle looked crestfallen. When Ms. Tolan nodded to her, she started down the aisle self-consciously. She tried to walk on her toes in order to seem taller, but she tripped over a piece of carpeting and stumbled.

"Michelle is blowing it in a major way," Heather observed. "Maybe you shouldn't have, like, said that right before her turn."

Suki yawned. "She didn't have a shot, anyway. I've been watching footage of the fashion shows. Forget Ms. Tolan's advice. Models walk completely differently. I've been practicing, and I know I'll blow Melvin away. He's not expecting to see a *professional* here."

It was Heather's turn next. She sailed down the aisle, her auburn hair gleaming and a big smile on her face. Obviously, she had no problem being looked at by a crowd of people. Melvin Fine gave a little clap when she finished.

"Bravo," he said.

Then it was Suki's turn. She slouched down the aisle, her hips thrust forward. A sulky, sexy pout was on her face. She looked like every fashion model Kelly had ever seen.

Kelly patiently waited for Suki to reach the end. She wasn't nervous at all. Not only had she done this before, but she didn't really want the job, anyway.

As Suki reached the end of the aisle, Kelly remembered the advice the designer Isidore Duncan had given her. It was simple and direct, just like Izzy. *Just love the clothes, Kelly. Then the audience will, too.* Kelly closed her eyes and told herself that her uniform was gorgeous. It was hard, but she screwed her eyes shut even tighter and told herself firmly that the gray skirt and white blouse were classic designs and any girl would feel beautiful in them.

When Ms. Tolan nodded at her, Kelly took off down the aisle with a big smile, telling herself how gracefully the pleated skirt swished against her legs and how crisp and white her blouse was. *Look at these clothes,* her walk seemed to say. *Aren't they fantastic?*

Melvin Fine nodded and smiled at her, and Kelly went off to join the waiting girls. She'd have loved to just slip out, but Ms. Tolan was by the door.

She'd done the best job she knew how to do, but she didn't expect anything. So Kelly almost passed out when, fifteen minutes later, Melvin Fine announced the three models he had picked: Andrea Young, Heather Henderson, and Kelly Kapowski.

"Wait a second," Suki said loudly, her face red. "That can't be right."

Mr. Fine swiveled and looked at her. "Why not?"

Suki walked over and lowered her voice. Since Kelly was standing right behind Mr. Fine, she heard every word.

"Do you know that my mother is chairing this benefit?" Suki asked furiously. "I'm Suki *Ballard.*"

Mr. Fine nodded. "How do you do, Miss Ballard," he said gravely.

"Well?" Suki said.

"Well, what?" Melvin Fine asked. His gray eyes were steely. Obviously, he didn't respond well to pressure.

"Maybe you want to reconsider," Suki said. She shifted from one foot to another, and Kelly saw that underneath her bravado, Suki was nervous. Mr. Fine could intimidate anyone.

"I've been picking models since before you were born, kiddo," Mr. Fine said softly. "Look, Suki, you're a beautiful girl. But I picked models to match my clothes. Easy elegance is my motto. The girls I picked combined looks and the most important thing—attitude."

Mr. Fine turned his back on Suki and said to Kelly, "I have a feeling you've modeled before. Am I right?"

Kelly nodded. "I was in Isidore Duncan's spring show in San Francisco," she admitted. "My girlfriend Lisa won a contest, and I wore her designs, not his. It was just a one-shot thing. I'm not a professional or anything."

"And how is Izzy?" Mr. Fine said. "He's one of my very favorite people."

"He's fantastic," Kelly agreed. "He was super nice to my friend Lisa."

Kelly began to tell Mr. Fine about her experience with Isidore Duncan. But she couldn't help noticing how Suki Ballard was looking at her. Somehow, Kelly had the uncomfortable feeling that she'd made a powerful enemy hate her even more than before.

▲   ▼   ▲

Zack rang the Neidermeyer doorbell. The gang waited, listening, while it chimed out a melody.

"Is that 'Can't Smile without You'?" Jessie asked.

"It sounded like 'Mandy' to me," Lisa said.

"I thought it was 'Stars and Stripes Forever,'" Screech volunteered.

The door opened, and Mrs. Neidermeyer stood there beaming at them. She was a plump woman with bouncy blond hair and a gingham apron over her dress. "Well, hello there," she said in a sweet voice.

"We're here to see Babette," Zack said, matching her wide smile. "Can she have visitors?"

"Well, now, how nice to see some of Babette's little friends come by," Mrs. Neidermeyer said. "She'll be so very pleased."

"Is she contagious?" Slater asked.

"No, no. Just don't let her sneeze on you, that's all," Mrs. Neidermeyer said, ushering them into a hallway wallpapered in a cheerful, pink-flowered print.

She led them to the foot of a rose-carpeted stairway. "Oh, Babette! Babette! Some of your nice friends from school are here to see you, honey." She turned to the group. "Just go on up; I know you kids like your privacy. It's the first door on the left."

Zack led the way. His sneakered feet seemed to sink into the lush carpet all the way up the stairs. He got to the first door on the left and knocked on it.

"Come in," Babette called.

They stepped through the doorway and stopped. It was like being inside a big bubble of Bazooka. The bubblegum-pink walls matched the pink-striped comforter and the pink window shades. A hot pink carpet was on the floor. Even Babette was dressed in a frilly pink bed jacket and had a big pink bow in her curly blond hair. She was lying in bed against pink and white lacy pillows, an open magazine on her lap.

"Hi," she said. Her light blue eyes shone. "Gee, it was nice of you guys to come and see me."

"You look great, Babette," Lisa said. "I'm glad to see you're not letting your fashion sense slide. Even when in bed, we can accessorize."

Babette nodded solemnly. "I couldn't agree with you more, Lisa."

"Babette, we're here for two reasons," Zack said. "The first is to see how you are, of course—"

Babette heaved a huge sigh. "Well, I could be better. I'm really achy, and my fever—"

"That's too bad," Zack said quickly. "The other reason has to do with Screech. The rumor around school is that you're worried he'll take your job."

Babette looked down and fingered a ruffle on her pillowcase. "Oh," she said.

"Babette, I just wanted to tell you that as soon as you're better, I'm going to step down," Screech said. "Scout's honor. Or treasurer's honor. Whatever. I promise."

"And Screech keeps his promises," Slater said.

"Besides, Babette," Jessie said soothingly, "nobody could fill your shoes."

With a glance at Babette's pink slippers, Zack decided that Jessie was definitely on the nose with that statement. Or should he say the toes? Judging by the size of her slippers, Babette's feet must be enormous.

"Gosh," Babette said. "I guess I was real worried about that."

"*How* worried?" Zack asked.

"Real, real worried," Babette said. She smiled. "But I'm not anymore. Everything's coming up roses."

And I bet they're pink, Zack thought. "So," he

said carefully, "if you did something or, uh, tried something so that Screech wouldn't stay on, you could, you know, undo it."

Babette looked guilty. "What do you mean?"

"Well," Jessie said, "say you did something impulsively that you didn't mean to do. Say you felt sorry about it."

"You guys are on to me, I can tell," Babette said with a deep sigh. "Okay, Screech. I'm really sorry. I didn't mean to do it."

"It's okay, Babette," Screech said. "I understand."

"Just give it to us," Zack said. "Nobody has to know anything."

Sniffing, Babette leaned over and reached underneath the white, lacy dust ruffle on the bottom of her bed. She slid out a book from underneath the bed. "Okay. Here's the official Bayside High senior class ledger with matching pen, Screech. I should have given it to you before. I just couldn't part with it." Tears slipped down Babette's pink cheeks.

"Wait a second," Jessie said. "You mean you didn't—"

"Come on, 'fess up," Screech said.

"We know that you—" Slater started.

"Thank you, Babette," Zack said, shooting a warning glance at the gang. Suddenly, he had started to feel sorry for Babette. Obviously, she took her job seriously. She would be crushed if she knew that someone had suspected her of stealing the money.

He took the ledger and handed it to Screech. "We hope you get better real soon."

"Thanks," Babette said. "I feel just awful."

"That's nice," Zack said, shutting the door behind them.

The gang filed out and went back downstairs. They refused Mrs. Neidermeyer's offer of cupcakes with strawberry icing and said good-bye. They found themselves out on the street in front of Babette's house.

"Why did you back off like that?" Jessie asked Zack.

Zack sighed. "Being class treasurer is Babette's whole life. I couldn't accuse her of stealing the money. She'd be destroyed."

"She really is sweet," Lisa said.

"I'll say," Slater said. "I'm getting a toothache."

"Did you see when she started to cry?" Jessie asked.

"You know, she could have just conned us good," Slater said. "That could have been a huge act to get us off the track."

"It could have been," Zack admitted.

Jessie shrugged. "So here we are. Back at square one."

"Square One?" Screech looked around. "Gosh, I thought we were on Poplar Circle."

Lisa groaned. "Will someone tell me again why we're *helping* this dweeb?"

Zack sighed and slung his arm around Screech's shoulders. "Because he's *our* dweeb," he said.

Chapter 9

▲ ▼ ▲ ▼ ▲

Kelly got to the Max later than usual, but the gang wasn't there. She didn't know if they'd already been and left, or if they'd gone somewhere else, or if they'd eventually show up. She slid into their regular booth and ordered a soda.

Things at Miss Fopp's had gone from bad to worse. Suki Ballard was telling everyone that the only reason Kelly had gotten the modeling job was that she'd gotten her friend Isidore Duncan to call Melvin Fine and insist he pick Kelly. Kelly didn't know if anyone really believed Suki or not. But it still didn't make for a terrific day at Miss Fopp's. Even Ivy Templeton had avoided her gaze.

Nancy Vance and Paul Wilson, two students from Bayside, came into the Max. Feeling blue, Kelly could barely summon up a smile as they passed her table.

Behind her, she heard Nancy say under her breath, "I guess Countess Kelly is missing her subjects."

"I'm surprised she even wants to hang out at the Max anymore," Paul said. "I heard she'll only eat in restaurants with linen tablecloths now."

Countess Kelly! Kelly felt her cheeks burn. Not only did she not have any friends at Miss Fopp's, now the kids at Bayside thought she was a snob! When she'd told them about how luxurious Miss Fopp's was, she hadn't told them to impress them. She'd just been trying to avoid telling everyone how miserable she was there.

Kelly wanted to burst into tears. She had to get out of Miss Fopp's. It was a school full of snobs, and people would think she was just like them. But how could she turn down all that money? How could she make her parents understand? She had to talk to Zack. She could always depend on him. Zack would find a way.

▲　　▼　　▲

The gang was still arguing about Babette when they reached the Max. As they started up the walk, Phyllis Ptowski rose from a bench near the entrance.

"Zack, can I talk to you?" she said.

"Sure," Zack said. "Go ahead, guys. I'll catch up."

Phyllis waited until the door closed behind the group. Then she turned to Zack. "I wanted to ask you something," she said. "My father got complimentary tickets to that new production at the Palisades Playhouse, and I was wondering if you'd like to go with me Saturday night." She said the words in a rush. Then she looked at him anxiously, twirling a curl of light brown hair.

"Phyllis, that sounds great," Zack said.

"Fantastic!" Phyllis burbled. "It starts at eight."

Zack shook his head. "But I can't. Thanks for thinking of me."

"Oh. Okay." Phyllis blushed and turned away. But as Zack headed for the door of the Max, she called to him. "Zack?"

He turned. "Yes?"

"Did you have fun on our date last Saturday?" Phyllis asked hesitantly.

He nodded. Phyllis's brown eyes looked soft and vulnerable. "I had a great time."

"Then why don't you want to go out with me again?" Phyllis blurted.

Zack took a few steps closer. "Phyllis, you know that I only go out with Kelly. Saturday night was just for the benefit of the senior class fund. I mean, I had fun. But I'm going steady with Kelly."

"But I thought that since she transferred out of Bayside..."

"Just because she doesn't go to Bayside doesn't mean she isn't still my girl," Zack said firmly.

To his surprise, a big tear suddenly rolled out of Phyllis's eye and trickled down her cheek. She looked embarrassed, too embarrassed to brush it away. Maybe she thought that if she didn't, Zack wouldn't notice it.

"Look, Phyllis, I think you're absolutely fantastic," Zack said gently. He reached over and wiped the tear from her cheek. "I just met Kelly first, that's all. I'm already in love with her. Once you fall in love, you're down for the count."

"I know," Phyllis said. Slowly, she smiled. "Thanks for being honest with me, Zack," she said softly.

"Some other guy will be lucky someday," Zack said. He leaned over and kissed her cheek.

And Kelly chose that moment to walk out the front door of the Max.

She stood there, feeling the breath knocked out of her from seeing Zack kiss another girl. But then, suddenly, Kelly was really able to look at the situation. Phyllis had been crying, she saw. She looked miserable, but happy, too.

And right then, Kelly saw things from Phyllis's perspective. She saw that Phyllis had been a nobody at Bayside, just because she weighed too much. She'd hung out with the kids who were too tall or too short or too heavy or too skinny. Anyone who looked different, who wasn't *cool*, was an automatic nerd. You were nice to nerds, but you didn't sit at their lunch table.

And suddenly, Kelly knew exactly how that felt.

"Sorry to interrupt," she said.

"Uh, Kelly—" Zack started nervously.

Kelly waved a hand. "It's okay, Zack. Hi, Phyllis."

"Hi," Phyllis said. She ducked her head and rushed past Kelly into the Max.

"Kelly, let me explain—" Zack started.

"You don't have to, Zack," Kelly said with a sigh. "Actually, I think I know exactly how Phyllis feels."

"What are you talking about?" Zack said.

"Try eating alone in the cafeteria sometime," Kelly said wryly. "It gives you a whole new perspective on things."

"Kelly, what's the matter?" Zack asked, looking into her face. "You've been so quiet this week."

Kelly sighed. "It's Miss Fopp's, Zack. It's just awful. I got on the wrong side of this snobby girl, and she's making my life miserable. None of the other girls will be friends with me. I don't know if I'd even *want* to be friends with them. I overhear conversations, and all I hear about is how much money a new outfit cost or which clubs they should join at Princeton next year. And if I have to take another deportment class, I'll scream! If this is what it's like to be rich, I'll pass."

Zack slipped his arm around Kelly. "It sounds like you've been having a rough time," he said sympathetically. "Why didn't you tell me?"

"I wanted to," Kelly said. "You guys are always talking about what's happening at Bayside. I feel so left out. Nobody talks to me at Miss Fopp's, but my friends here don't really talk to me, either. You guys treat me like a different person. I called Jessie last night, and her mother said that she was shopping at the mall with Lisa. They didn't even ask me! They think I'll only shop at expensive boutiques now."

"I'm sorry, Kelly," Zack said. "Maybe we *have*

treated you differently. And things sound pretty awful at Miss Fopp's. It's hard to adjust to a new school. But it will get better."

"But, Zack, I don't think it will," Kelly brooded. "I don't *like* it there. It's just not me. I don't think the money is worth being unhappy, do you?" She gazed up at him, her blue eyes troubled.

"I'm not sure," Zack said. "I mean, if you just get through a few months at Miss Fopp's, you don't have to worry about your college education."

"I know," Kelly said. "But somehow I have the feeling that if I keep going to school there, I'll turn into a person I don't want to be. Does that sound crazy?"

"Well..."

"It's like I have this choice," Kelly said thoughtfully. "I can be *me*, Kelly Kapowski, or I can turn into this other person."

"I like the old Kelly just fine," Zack said. "But I have to admit that I like that the *new* Kelly doesn't have to break her neck working at the Yogurt 4-U."

"Even the Yogurt 4-U is starting to look pretty good to me," Kelly said ruefully. "At least I *earned* that money. I didn't have to change myself to get it."

"Wait a second," Zack said, confused. "You're telling me that you *miss* working after school and on weekends?"

"In a way, I do," Kelly said slowly.

"That *is* crazy," Zack said.

"The thing is, Zack, I feel trapped," Kelly said with a frown. "Marion will flip if I say I want to transfer back to Bayside. I just know I'd lose everything. How can I tell my parents? They're counting on me now. And all my brothers and sisters are counting on me, too."

"Hold the phone," Zack said. "Are you seriously thinking of dropping out?"

"Isn't that what we're talking about?" Kelly asked.

"I thought you were just blowing off steam," Zack said. "Kelly, you can't drop out. Just think of all that money. What's a little high school anguish compared to that? You can do it, kiddo. Keep your chin up. Look for the silver lining—or should I say the gold. It's always darkest before the dawn. Opportunity knocks. Don't be cruel to a heart that's true—"

"Zack!" Kelly pushed herself away from him. "You haven't been listening to me at all. I'm miserable!"

"I know," Zack said. "But you're miserable and *rich*. Don't you know heiresses are always miserable? Look at Princess Di."

"You can't even *see* me anymore," Kelly said angrily. "All you see are dollar signs. I'm telling you how unhappy I am, and you don't even care!"

"Kelly, of course I care!" Zack protested.

"That's probably why you aren't chasing after Phyllis," Kelly said. "It has nothing to do with me, Kelly Kapowski. It has to do with Countess Kelly. You don't want to jeopardize your financial future, right?"

"That's not fair," Zack said, hurt. "How can you say that?"

"Because that's how you're acting, Zack!" Kelly

cried, her eyes filling with tears. "You haven't been the same since you found out about Marion, and neither has anyone else. I hate having this money! And I hate you, too!" Kelly ran off, her long hair flying.

▲   ▼   ▲

Zack shook his head several times, trying to clear it. Had Kelly just said that she *hated* him? He must have heard wrong. Kelly would never say something so terrible. She was just upset. Probably she was more upset over seeing him kiss Phyllis than she would admit. He'd call her later tonight and smooth things over. Now he had some detecting to do.

He pushed open the door of the Max. The gang was sipping sodas, eating nachos, and talking in low voices. It looked like another strategy session, and he was definitely needed.

"Any new developments?" he asked, taking a chip loaded with cheese and guacamole.

"We're going over the list of people who had access to the student council room again," Jessie said. "We're trying to figure out if any of them has suddenly started spending a lot of money."

"But even if we *do* figure it out, we still can't figure out how they got in the cash drawer," Slater said. He took another chip and ate it. "I'd say that's our main problem."

"Screech, are you *sure* you never let that key out of your sight?" Lisa asked.

Screech nodded. "I'm positive." He reached inside his shirt and drew out the key on a long chain. "It's been close to my heart since I got it. And I'm sure Mr. Belding is careful with his key, too."

Everyone looked at Screech.

"Mr. Belding has a key?" Zack said incredulously. "Why didn't you tell us that before?"

"I didn't think it was important," Screech said with a shrug. "I mean, it's not like Mr. B could be the thief."

There was a long pause.

"True," Lisa said.

"Right," Jessie said.

"Of course not," Zack said.

"No way," Slater said.

Then they looked at each other.

"Could he?" Lisa asked in a small voice.

Chapter 10

▲ ▼ ▲ ▼ ▲

"Mrs. B really screwed up their finances," Slater said. "So Mr. Belding is under a lot of financial pressure."

"They repossessed his car," Lisa said.

"So his credit is completely shot," Zack said.

"And Old Pete needs an operation," Jessie said.

"He said the hospital wouldn't accept his credit," Screech said. "But the other day he told me that Old Pete *was* going to have the operation."

"So he could have put down a deposit or something," Slater said.

"He could have felt that he had no choice," Lisa said.

They looked at each other.

"Nah," they all said together.

They sat silent for a minute, letting it all sink in. Mr. Belding, a thief? It wasn't possible. But then again, desperate people can do desperate things. Hadn't they been saying that all week?

"It can't be," Zack said.

"No, it can't," Slater agreed.

"But it *might*," Lisa said.

"Well, if it *is* true," Zack said, "we have a major problem. What are we going to do about it?"

"One of us will have to go to him and ask him to confess," Jessie decided. "If we all barge in, he might be intimidated. But one person might get him to open up. The person will swear that the secret will be safe."

"That sounds tricky," Slater said. "What if Mr. Belding didn't do it? He'll be really mad. He'll probably suspend the person for making false accusations."

"It's a tough job, but somebody's got to do it," Jessie insisted.

"But who?" Lisa asked. "I'd do it, but I just know I'd blow it. It needs someone who's super sensitive. Someone Mr. Belding trusts."

"That counts Zack out," Slater joked.

"Maybe it *should* be me," Zack said. "After all, I've spent more time with Mr. Belding than anyone."

"It wasn't exactly *quality* time, Zack," Jessie pointed out.

Screech straightened. "I'll do it," he said. "It's my problem, and I have to be the one to solve it. Besides, I'm supposed to meet with him tomorrow afternoon, anyway, to resign my position. Unless he fires me first. Gosh, if we're wrong about his being a thief, there might be a firing squad!"

"Don't be ridiculous, Screech," Lisa said. Then she slipped off the scarf around her neck and handed it to him. "But here's a blindfold, just in case."

▲   ▼   ▲

That night, Kelly heard the phone ring. A moment later, her brother Kerry knocked on her door. She put down her pen and sighed. "I told you, I'm not home," she called.

He peeked around the door, a respectful look on his freckled face. "It's Mrs. Lenihan."

"Oh." Kelly stomped down the hall in her fluffy slippers and picked up the phone. "Hi, Aunt Marion," she said.

"How are things going, Kelly?"

"Everything's going fine," Kelly said shortly.

"Are you wearing my pearls like you promised?"

"Every day," Kelly answered honestly. She *was* wearing them every day—under her sweater.

"Now, details. Have you made any friends?"

Kelly didn't like to admit that she hadn't. "Uh, this girl Ivy Templeton is nice."

"Templeton? Her father isn't that Nathaniel Templeton, who was president of the Silver Birch Savings and Loan?"

"I think so. Ivy mentioned he was involved in some bank or something."

"Well, drop her immediately, Kelly. She is *not* someone you should be associating with. What if her father goes to jail?"

It would be easy to drop Ivy, Kelly thought. Because Ivy had already dropped her. Oh, Ivy smiled at her when she was sure Suki wasn't looking. And today she'd even said hello. But Ivy had never tried to eat lunch with Kelly again.

In any case, Kelly didn't like Marion telling her to drop Ivy.

"Now, tell me some other news," Marion said.

"Well, I got picked to be in some stupid fashion show benefit at the Beverly Grande Hotel."

"Fabulous! It's the biggest society benefit of the year out there. Who's chairing the event?"

"Mrs. Somebody Ballard. Her daughter goes to Miss Fopp's."

"Mrs. Ballard...wait—is she Mrs. Wendell Ballard?"

Kelly studied her nails. "Yes, that sounds like it."

"Marvelous! The Ballards are one of the very few socially prominent families in Los Angeles. I'm glad you're getting to know them."

"Actually," Kelly said, "I'm not, really. Suki Ballard is a total nimrod."

"Excuse me, Kelly? Would you mind speaking the English language, please? You know I don't like that surfer talk."

"She's not a nice girl," Kelly said. There was plenty she could say about Suki, but she didn't like to talk about people behind their backs, no matter how awful they were. The nimrod comment had just slipped out.

"Nonsense, I'm sure she's lovely. Amanda Ballard is one of the most cultured women in Los Angeles. Now, Kelly, I want you to befriend this Suki. I think she would be a perfect best friend for you."

"No way, Aunt Marion," Kelly said firmly. "I'm sorry, I can't. Even if I wanted to. Suki and I got off on the wrong foot."

"So get on the right one, dear. Do you understand?" Suddenly, Marion's voice acquired a steely quality.

Kelly caught her breath. It was one thing for Marion to suggest that she wear her stupid jewelry. But this was something else. "I'm sorry, Aunt Marion," she said quietly. "But I won't let anyone tell me who to be friends with. Or who *not* to be friends with. That's just the way it is."

"Kelly, I don't think I like what I'm hearing," Marion said in a frosty tone. "Surely you realize that I'm entitled to guide you—"

"Guide me? Maybe," Kelly said. "Dictate to me—no way, José."

"Now, young lady, I don't like to be called José. I don't like that at all."

"I'm sorry, Aunt Marion. It's just an expression. But I meant what I said." Kelly sighed. "Listen, I really have to go. I have all this deportment homework to do. It was real nice talking to you. 'Bye, now."

Kelly replaced the receiver quietly. She stood, staring at the phone, thinking about her conversation with Marion.

"I don't want to be friends with the *right* people," she murmured. "I don't even *like* the right people."

Kelly thought about the fashion show on Saturday. It would be crammed full of the "right" people, and she would be miserable. Why was she doing it, anyway? She was the only one of the girls whose mother hadn't been invited to participate with her daughter. She was supposed to be the partner of some society woman who didn't have any children. Ms. Tolan had told her that Kelly would be modeling matching Melvin Fine suits with some big shot named Mrs. Charles Abernathy. Suddenly, Kelly realized that she'd been conned. The fashion show organizers probably didn't want Minnie Kapowski, legal secretary, as one of the models. Kelly's mother hadn't even been *invited* to the show at all.

Why was she going to some snooty function that was excluding her own mother?

Kelly felt rebellion stir inside her. Tomorrow, she decided, she would tell Ms. Tolan that she was dropping out of the fashion show. Suki would say it was true that Kelly'd only gotten the job because of Isidore Duncan's influence, but Kelly didn't care. And if Aunt Marion didn't like it, it was just too bad.

Just then, the phone rang under her fingers. She let it ring. She knew it was Zack, and for once, he was the last person in the world she wanted to talk to. He just didn't understand what she was going through. He didn't want to. He was only thinking about the money.

Kerry stuck his head out of the doorway of his room. "Are you going to answer that?" he said.

"No," Kelly said, turning away. "And if it's Zack, tell him I'm not home."

Kerry frowned. "Again?"

"Again," Kelly said firmly. Then she shut her bedroom door.

▲   ▼   ▲

Zack hung up the receiver. It was the third time Kerry had told him that Kelly wasn't home. It didn't take a genius to figure out that Kelly was still angry at him. Obviously, making up with her was going to be harder than he'd thought.

Why had his girlfriend picked this time to hold a grudge? Zack had enough to think about, with Mr. Belding biting the dust right before his eyes.

He still had a hard time believing that Mr. Belding could be the culprit. He knew better than anyone how honest and straightforward Mr. Belding was. Mr. Belding didn't believe in cutting corners. As the premiere corner-cutter of Bayside, Zack knew that from personal experience. Mr. B's notion of right and wrong was steady as a rock. He always followed the rules.

He tried to picture Mr. Belding's position. His credit was gone, and he needed to pay the medical expenses for someone close to him. Who would blame him for succumbing to temptation? He had been worried about Old Pete, and the money was irresistible.

Money was the biggest temptation in the world, Zack mused. It could even reach out and snare Mr. Belding, make him do something that was totally against his character. It was downright scary.

Zack thought about Kelly. If money could do that to Mr. Belding, what could it do to Kelly? Maybe that's what she'd been trying to tell him today. Maybe it was too much for her to handle. Maybe she didn't *like* what she saw at Miss Fopp's, and she was scared it would happen to her. She'd been scared and unhappy, and he hadn't even listened to her!

Zack felt like a fool. Now he saw that every time she complained, he had told her it didn't matter. He had told her that the money was the most important thing. No wonder Kelly hated him! He was a complete jerk!

Zack reached for the phone again, but he knew that Kelly wouldn't talk to him. It was too late to call, anyway.

Zack flopped back on his bed and stared at the ceiling. How could he win Kelly back? Since she never wanted to see him again, it could be kind of difficult. She wouldn't come to the phone, and he'd bet that if he showed up at her door, one of her burly brothers would tell him she wasn't home. He'd have to find another way.

▲   ▼   ▲

The next day, Zack, Slater, Jessie, and Lisa sat gloomily at their table in the cafeteria. They picked at their sandwiches halfheartedly.

"I'm so bummed about Mr. Belding," Jessie said with a sigh.

"Me, too," Slater said. "I've completely lost my appetite."

"Wow," Lisa said. "If Slater loses his appetite, I *know* things are bad."

Just then, Screech ran into the cafeteria. Bypassing an IMPEACH SCREECH! sign, he skidded to a stop in front of their table.

"Screech, what is it?" Lisa said. "You look like you've seen a ghost."

"No," Screech said, "But I *have* seen the senior class fund. It's back in the drawer!"

"Are you sure?" Zack said.

"Of course I'm sure!" Screech exclaimed. Then he lowered his voice and sank into a chair. "Every penny," he said. "Do you think Mr. B knew we were on to him?"

The gang exchanged puzzled glances. "This is so weird," Jessie said. "Our problem has been solved—sort of. I mean, the crime still happened. Should we just drop it, or what?"

Zack frowned. "The thing is, if it *was* Mr. Belding, he must be in real trouble to do something like that. Just because he returned the money doesn't mean we shouldn't talk to him. Maybe when you go to see him, you should feel him out, Screech."

Screech nodded earnestly. "I *was* planning to hug him," he said. "In a manly way, of course."

"I mean get him to talk to you," Zack explained. "Find out if he's in trouble or not."

"Okay, Zack," Screech said. "When it comes to sensitive man-to-man talks, I'm your guy. I mean, I'm your sensitive man."

Zack crumpled his napkin and stood up. "Good luck, Screech. Well, I've got to motor. I've got a man-to-woman talk to take care of myself. I've got to talk to Kelly."

"Kelly?" Jessie asked. "But she's at Miss Fopp's."

"I know," Zack said.

"What are you going to do—just walk in?" Slater asked in disbelief.

"You'll be awfully conspicuous," Jessie said.

"They'll spot you in a second," Lisa agreed. "You're not exactly the image of a Miss Fopp's girl."

"I'll take my chances," Zack declared. "Kelly's worth the risk."

Chapter 11

▲ ▼ ▲ ▼ ▲

It was easier than Zack thought to get into Miss Fopp's. He found a side door and waited behind a tree until two seniors sneaked out, giggling, to run to the corner store. They left the door propped open with a rock, so Zack just slipped right in.

He found himself in a hallway. It was carpeted in red, and closed oak doors were on either side of him. Portraits of gray-faced old ladies lined the long hall. Their beady eyes seemed to be watching him. Zack whistled under his breath. This was a school? It looked more like a haunted house.

Even while classes were going on, Bayside was always full of noise—the orchestra was practicing, or kids were laughing in Ms. McCracken's class, or Mr. Monza, the head of maintenance, was whistling as he passed through the halls. The school was full of big windows that let in light and air. Miss Fopp's school seemed as though a window hadn't been cracked open in sixty years.

Zack padded down the thickly carpeted hallway. He'd better think of something quick before he was thrown out on his ear. The gang had been right. He was completely conspicuous. He'd been hoping that he could pose as a maintenance guy, or say he was from the phone company. But somehow, Zack knew now that it wouldn't work.

Suddenly, he heard footsteps coming from ahead of him, around a corner. Zack had no choice—he leaped toward the closest door, listened a moment to make sure it wasn't a classroom, and then eased it open and slipped inside.

He had landed in the nurse's office, Zack saw at once. Luckily, it was empty. There was a desk facing him and a white screen on wheels that divided the room in half. On a chair were a gray wool skirt, a blazer, and a small beret. Then Zack heard the sound of sheets rustling.

"Nurse Richardson?" a plaintive voice called. "Do I have to keep lying here? I'm not feeling dizzy anymore, I promise. It's just because I skipped breakfast and then ran up three flights of stairs. I really do feel better. Nurse Richardson?"

Zack didn't hesitate. He snatched the skirt, blazer, and beret and quietly left the nurse's office again. As soon as he was in the hall, he jumped into the skirt and buttoned it. Luckily, the sick girl must have been a little plump, because it fit perfectly. He slipped off his jeans underneath the skirt and then put on the blazer and beret. He looked down at his legs in sweat socks and high top sneakers. He had the perfect disguise. He looked like a rich, ugly nerd with hairy legs.

From somewhere, a bell rang, and Zack jumped. Classes were about to change! He heard the sound of doors opening, and Zack panicked. He reached for the door on his right and peeked inside. It was a library, with thick velvet curtains and deep armchairs. Perfect. He could turn one of the chairs around and hide in it until everyone had changed classes. Then he'd hunt for Kelly again.

Zack bundled up his jeans and shoved them underneath a red velvet sofa. Then he settled himself into a big armchair in a far corner. He tucked his legs underneath, grabbed a book from the table next to him, and leaned his head on his hand. If anyone noticed him, they'd think he or, hopefully, she was either asleep or concentrating.

He was just in time. He heard the door open, and a trio of girls walked in.

"Hurry up, Suki," an auburn-haired girl said. "We only have five minutes before class."

"I swear, Henderson," a bored voice said. "You're going to give me a heart attack."

"Did you hear that Kapowski dropped out of the fashion show?" the auburn-haired girl, who Suki had called Henderson, said in a low voice.

"And I know why," Suki said. "She's totally

humiliated about using her friendship with Isidore Duncan to snag the job. She just couldn't face it."

"So you were right all along," the short, dark-haired girl said with a sigh.

"Of course," Suki said.

"Never mind that," Henderson said. "We want to hear all about your date last night."

Zack peeked between his fingers as the three girls settled on the red couch. He couldn't believe what a nasty girl that Suki was. No wonder Kelly hated it here! Zack's adrenaline was pumping. He would love to stand up and give that girl a piece of his mind. And it would be a piece large enough to smash her to smithereens.

"The date was fabulous, as usual," Suki said. "Mr. Denny Vane is *extremely* cool."

Zack frowned. Mr. Denny Vane? Could she be talking about Bayside's very own hood wannabe? She sure didn't look like Denny's type. She didn't even look like she had *one* tattoo.

"Remember I told you that he wanted to get the watch he gave me engraved? Well, I gave it back to him on Wednesday night and he gave it back to me last night. Look." Suki slipped off the watch and held it out. "It says ALWAYS, BABE. Is that like the most romantic thing you ever heard?"

"Gosh," the dark-haired girl breathed. "Totally."

But Henderson leaned closer and looked at Suki's wrist instead of the watch. "What's that on your wrist, Suki? It's like some totally gross skin disease."

"Eewwww," the other girl said.

Suki examined her wrist. "Gross! It's *green*."

"That's not a gold watch," Henderson said matter-of-factly. "It's a fake."

"Dream on, Heather," Suki said. "Denny wouldn't give me a *fake* watch. Besides, when he gave it to me, I showed it to my mother, and she told me it was real. Nobody can fool Amanda Ballard when it comes to jewelry."

"Then why is your wrist green?" Heather Henderson asked stubbornly.

"Maybe it *is* some totally gross skin disease or, like, something awful like that," the other girl wailed.

Suki tossed her blond hair. "You girls are so immature. If you don't shut up, I'll make you hang out with Kapowski."

Zack wanted to get up and sock Suki in the nose, but he didn't. A light bulb had gone on over his head.

Zack snapped the book shut and walked out of the library, keeping his face away from the trio on the couch. It was incredible and, like, totally weird, but here at Miss Fopp's, he'd solved the Bayside heist!

▲   ▼   ▲

Kelly took her seat as Ms. Tolan bustled into deportment class, her hands full of papers. Everyone quieted and sat up with the correct posture: shoulders straight, knees together, ankles crossed. Sneaking a look at her neighbor for pointers, Kelly tried to cross her ankles and kicked herself in the shin.

"Miss Kapowski," Ms. Tolan said.

Kelly couldn't help shrinking a little in her chair. Every day, she made a major mistake. What would it be this time?

"Ankles crossed to the side, not in front of you," Ms. Tolan said. "As I was saying. I'm passing back your homework assignment, which was to thank a friend for a lovely birthday gift."

She held up a familiar-looking paper by the tips of her fingers. Kelly groaned inwardly. It was her paper.

"Miss Kapowski, you have given us an excellent example of how *not* to write a thank-you note." Ms. Tolan frowned at the paper. "'Dear Jessie: You are the coolest ever. Thanks for the fab-u-loso sweatshirt. I'm a total "Star Trek" hound, and "Beam me up, Scotty" is my favorite expression. Yours 'till the kitchen sinks, Kelly.'"

The class burst out laughing, and Ms. Tolan looked over her half-glasses at Kelly. "What do you call this?"

"You said it could be informal," Kelly said.

"This is not *informal*, Miss Kapowski. This is *subhuman*. Now, let me read Miss Ballard's note—"

A sharp knock sounded on the library door, and Ms. Tolan stopped. "Come in."

A familiar-looking student walked in and handed a note to Ms. Tolan. Kelly frowned. The girl was stocky and muscular, and short blond hair stuck out from underneath a gray beret. Kelly's gaze traveled downward and discovered that this familiar student had very hairy legs.

Ms. Tolan peered at the girl. "I don't think I know you."

"I'm new," the girl said in a high-pitched voice. "I'm Zackarella Morris."

Kelly looked over and met twinkling hazel eyes. It was Zack! She didn't know whether to scream or to burst out laughing.

"Miss Kapowski, you're to report to the administration office at once," Ms. Tolan said.

She stood up. "Yes, Ms. Tolan." Trying not to giggle, she followed Zack from the room. She was still angry at him, but who could stay mad at a guy wearing a gray wool skirt?

"Nice legs, Morris," she said when they got outside.

He grinned. "Now do you believe me when I say I'd do anything for you?"

Kelly laughed. "I'll never doubt it again."

"Is there somewhere we can talk?"

"Sure," Kelly said. She led Zack to the small room off the dining hall that was sometimes used for Future Socialites of America meetings. She closed the door behind them.

"Kelly, I just had to see you," Zack said in a rush. "I had to tell you that I've been a jerk. I don't care about the money. I care about you. If you want to tell Marion to go jump in the lake, I'll be the first one to push her off the dock." He looked at her, his hazel eyes sincere. "I love you."

Kelly sighed. "Oh, Zack, I know that. I'm just so confused about everything."

"Look, Kelly," Zack said, taking her hands. "I don't know what you should do. But I want you to know that whatever you decide, I'll support you."

"Thanks, Zack," Kelly said softly. "That means a lot." She stepped into his arms, and they hugged.

When they drew apart, Zack said, "Now, I have to tell you something. The most incredible thing happened while I was looking for you, Kelly."

"What?" Kelly asked. She giggled. "You discovered that gray is your color?"

"I discovered who stole the Bayside student fund," Zack declared. "Denny Vane."

Kelly gasped. "Denny? How do you know?"

"I overheard that girl he's dating—Suzi? Suet?"

"Suki," Kelly said with a groan.

"She said that Denny gave her a gold watch. And you and I know that Denny doesn't have any money. He's known as the moocher of Bayside High. He's always scaring little freshmen into lending him money."

"That's true," Kelly said slowly. "But he could have gotten a job or something."

"Denny Vane? Let's have a reality check. But here's the clincher, Kelly. Denny took *back* the watch to get it engraved. Or so he said. But when he gave it back to Suki last night, her wrist turned green."

Kelly frowned. "So?"

"So he gave her back a *fake* watch."

"But why?" Kelly asked, confused. "And how does that prove that Denny got the money from the class fund?"

"Because he gave the money *back*," Zack explained. "Screech found all of it in the desk drawer this morning. So Denny must have felt guilty and sold the watch, and then bought a cheap replacement."

"Wait a second," Kelly said. "How did he get the key to the student council room? And the drawer? Did he steal Babette's purse?"

"No," Zack said. "She really *did* misplace her purse that time. She wasn't feeling well, and she was probably feeling kind of fuzzy. It wasn't a premeditated thing. Denny just saw his opportunity and took it."

"But when?" Kelly asked. "And how?"

"Remember I told you how we all collided in the hall outside the gym during the dance?"

"Right," Kelly said, smiling. "You pretended to have amnesia, and Mr. Belding almost called an ambulance. He was pretty mad."

"But before that, Denny collided with Mr. Belding," Zack explained. "I remembered hearing the chains on his motorcycle jacket clank. But it was actually Mr. Belding's keys falling out of his pocket. I led Mr. Belding away before he noticed. But Denny must have seen them. He already knew that Screech was about to lock the money in the drawer. So he waited until

Screech got back to the dance, and then went and stole it. And he put the keys back when—"

"Wait," Kelly interrupted. "I know. When we all did the limbo, Mr. Belding took off his jacket and draped it on a chair. Denny could have returned the keys then."

"Exactly!" Zack said.

Kelly sighed. "Poor Denny. It must have been hard for him to fall for a rich girl like Suki. She probably demanded things that he couldn't deliver, and he was afraid of losing her."

Zack shook his head in admiration. "If I didn't already think you were the sweetest girl in the world, you just proved it once again," he said, hugging her. "You even forgive a hood like Denny Vane. Pretty soon, you'll be forgiving a witch like Suki."

"Don't push it," Kelly said with a laugh.

"Poor Mr. Belding," Zack said. "He was on our list of suspects. We talked ourselves into thinking he was the thief."

"Mr. Belding? He wouldn't steal time," Kelly scoffed. "At least you didn't confront him about it. Be grateful for *that.*"

"Oops," Zack said.

Kelly looked at him nervously. "Oh, Zack. Don't tell me."

"Screech has a meeting with him after fifth period," Zack groaned. "He's going to talk to him. He promised to handle it delicately. He's not supposed to come out and accuse him or anything."

"Screech? Handle something delicately?" Kelly asked incredulously. "That's like using a fire hydrant to put out a match. We'd better get over there and stop him."

"We?" Zack asked.

"I'm still a Bayside student at heart," Kelly said. "And Screech is my friend."

"But you'd be cutting school," Zack said. "Isn't Miss Fopp's really strict? I'd hate to get on the wrong side of that Ms. Tolan. Not that she even *has* a right side."

"Who cares about Ms. Tolan? Come on." Kelly grabbed Zack's hand. "Stop talking and start running. Just don't trip over your hem."

▲ ▼ ▲

In Mr. Belding's office, Screech nervously gripped the arms of his chair. He hoped he was up to the job. He just had to help Mr. Belding. The principal had helped them all out so many times.

"I'm glad the money was returned, Screech," Mr. Belding said. "Maybe we should just put it all behind us."

"I agree, Mr. Belding. Absolutely. But if I *could* talk to the thief, I'd thank him for returning the money. And then I'd ask him if there was a problem that he just couldn't handle by himself. And then I'd offer to help."

"That's very broad-minded of you, Screech," Mr.

Belding said. "After all, this person got you into hot water."

"But maybe they didn't mean to," Screech said. "Maybe that person was desperate. Maybe they didn't have anyone to talk to."

Mr. Belding nodded. "That's very compassionate of you, Screech."

"So, what do you say, Mr. Belding?" Screech asked desperately. Mr. Belding wasn't getting the hint. He was awfully thick. "I think we need a sensitive, man-to-man talk. It's time we bonded and did some serious sharing."

"Sharing? What do you want?" Mr. Belding asked, alarmed. "My tie?" His hand closed over it protectively.

Screech looked him in the eye. "I want to know your feelings, Mr. Belding."

"Is this some sort of psychology project?" Mr. Belding asked suspiciously.

"Pretend I'm not a student," Screech said. "Pretend I'm a friend. Pretend I'm a friend talking to a friend with a problem. Pretend that friend with a problem ripped off the other friend because he had nowhere else to turn. Pretend that the other friend understood the friend and wanted the friend to understand—"

Mr. Belding groaned. "This is worse than talking to Zack."

Just then, Screech heard a weird noise. "Mr. Belding, what's that noise?"

"Oh, that's just Old Pete," Mr. Belding said. "He's under my desk taking a nap."

"You make your *grandfather* sleep under your desk?" Screech asked. Tears sprang to his eyes. "Are you really that poor, Mr. Belding?"

"I'm not poor, Screech, and Old Pete isn't my grandfather. He's my dog. Look."

Screech leaned over and peered underneath the desk. There was a basset hound sleeping near Mr. Belding's feet. He opened one eye, snorted, and went back to sleep again.

"Hey! Old Pete's a dog!" Screech exclaimed.

"Of course he's a dog," Mr. Belding said.

"You mean you went to all that trouble for a *dog*?" Screech blurted. "Mr. Belding, you're my hero! You should go down in the Animal Lovers' Hall of Fame! I see it now. You and Old Pete right next to Michael Jackson and his monkey."

"What do you mean, go to all that trouble?" Mr. Belding said. "All I did was take him to the animal hospital."

"But you *paid* for it," Screech said. "And your credit was shot. You didn't have any money. You risked your reputation to save Pete!"

Mr. Belding's frown got even deeper. "What do you mean, I risked my—"

"It's okay. I understand completely," Screech babbled. "You were always going to pay it back. You just *borrowed* it."

"Borrowed what?"

Screech opened his mouth to say "the senior class fund," but a hand clapped over it.

"Hi, Mr. Belding," Zack said. "It's great to see you, sir. Just thought we'd stop by and say hello. You're looking great. We have to get to class now."

Mr. Belding looked Zack up and down, from the tip of his beret to the hem of his gray wool skirt. "I'd say you should be getting to a psychiatrist instead, Morris. You've really gone off the deep end this time."

Ruff! agreed Old Pete.

Chapter 12

▲ ▼ ▲ ▼ ▲

On Monday morning, Kelly took her seat in deportment class. She sat like Kelly Kapowski, not Countess Kelly. Both her feet were on the floor, and her ankles were most definitely *not* crossed. Ms. Tolan frowned disapprovingly at her. But Kelly wasn't afraid of Ms. Tolan anymore.

"I have the homework assignments here," she said. "Miss Kapowski, since you disappeared not only from class but also from school on Friday, I do not have an assignment from you. I don't know whether to consider that a blessing or not. But I must tell you that I was *extremely* disappointed not to see you at the charity luncheon fashion show on Saturday." Ms. Tolan's thin lips pressed together in disapproval. "Thank goodness Miss Ballard was able to fill in for you at the last minute."

"Ms. Tolan?" Suki raised her hand. "I think you're being hard on Kelly. Everybody knows that, well, she's a charity student herself. I mean, her mother is a legal *secretary*. It's not like Mrs. Kapowski could have been involved in the show. My mother knew she'd feel completely out of place. And Kelly would have, too. I think we should be supportive of her decision."

Kelly felt anger sweep over her. She was sick and tired of being patronized and insulted by Suki Ballard.

"I don't know what I'd do without your support, Suki," Kelly said brightly. "And I'm sure it really helped Melvin Fine see the light when your mother called him and told him she wouldn't wear his designs for the next thirty years if he didn't put you in the show." Ivy had told her that piece of information this morning. Mrs. Templeton had overheard Mrs. Ballard bragging about it at the luncheon. Mrs. Ballard had been delighted at how she'd used her influence to get her daughter into the show.

A murmur of interested chatter went through the class.

"Gee, Suki," Kelly continued sweetly, "I hope you didn't mind being chosen by blackmail. I'm supportive of your decision to go ahead and do the show, anyway."

Suki actually blushed. Then she looked furious. She opened her mouth and closed it again. *Amazing,* Kelly thought, grinning. *Suki Ballard is actually at a loss for words.* Looking around, she saw that every girl in class was trying not to laugh, even Heather and Michelle.

"Ms. Tolan," Kelly said, standing up, "I only came to class today to say good-bye. Miss Rumson kicked me out this morning. Apparently, I'm not Miss Fopp material." She glanced at Suki and her friends. "I've never been so happy about anything in my life."

"Well," Ms. Tolan said. "I see. I hadn't given up hope on you, Miss Kapowski. But Miss Rumson knows best. Just don't forget what you learned here. Etiquette comes first."

"Right," Kelly said. "Later!"

As she started down the hall, Kelly heard a "Pssst" behind her. Ivy Templeton ran toward her.

"You really gave it to Suki," she said admiringly. "I wish you were staying, Kelly! I feel really bad about being such a complete wimp. I should have stood up to her and been your friend. But weak moral character runs in the family."

"Well, it can stop with you, Ivy," Kelly said, "if you want it to. If you ask me, the rest of the school is hoping that somebody stands up to Suki. Why shouldn't that someone be you?"

"Because I have everything to lose," Ivy said.

"You might lose a few friends like Heather or Shannon," Kelly said. "But who needs them?"

Ivy looked thoughtful. "You know, Mrs. Ballard totally snubbed my mom at that fashion show. The Ballards aren't going to help my parents, no matter what I do."

"Ivy, you have to live your own life," Kelly told her. "My dad always says that you have to look yourself in the mirror every morning. Not your parents, or your friends, or anybody else. You have to be able to look yourself in the eye and say, 'I did the best I could.'"

"Your dad sounds pretty smart," Ivy said.

"And he's only a *foreman*," Kelly teased. She gave Ivy an impulsive hug. "Good-bye, Ivy. And good luck."

"Thanks," Ivy said. "I'm sorry to see you go, Kelly. Miss Fopp's needs people like you."

"Well, you'll just have to take my place," Kelly said.

"I'll do my best," Ivy promised.

▲　▼　▲

When Zack got to school that day, he spotted Denny locking up his motorcycle. Motioning to the gang to come with him, he headed for Denny.

Denny was about four inches taller than Zack. He wasn't as muscular as Slater, but he looked wiry and strong. He gazed at them with cool, flat eyes. Screech ducked behind Lisa, but the rest of them stood their ground.

"To what do I owe this great honor?" he asked flippantly. "You guys selling Girl Scout cookies?"

"We know what you did, Denny," Zack said.

"Whoa, I'm shaking," Denny said. "What do you think you know that I did?"

"You stole the senior class fund," Jessie said, her eyes flashing.

"Don't bother to deny it," Lisa said.

Screech popped out from behind her shoulder. "Yeah," he said.

Denny hesitated. His eyes flicked from one serious face to another. "Why should I?" he said finally with a careless shrug. "It's no big deal. I didn't steal it—I borrowed it. I put the money back."

"It's still a crime, Denny," Zack said.

Denny shrugged. "According to who? I repeat, Morris. It's no big deal."

"If it's no big deal, you won't mind if we tell Mr. Belding what we know," Jessie said.

Denny looked nervous. "Hey, wait a second, you guys. I've been suspended five times this year already. If I get caught doing something else wrong, I get expelled. I'm finally going to get my diploma this year, and my mom is counting on it. She has a bad heart, you know," Denny concluded.

"Give us a break, Vane," Zack said, rolling his eyes.

"Okay, okay. But my dad will kick me from here to New York if I get expelled, okay?"

The gang hesitated. "It was wrong," Screech said, coming out from behind Lisa. "And you nearly got me impeached."

Denny leaned against his motorcycle. "Look, let

me tell you what happened. I met this girl. I'm talking class, guys. She's the best thing that ever happened to me. I had to impress her." He spread his hands. "You don't know what it's like being me. You should see the *dates* I get. It would give you nightmares." Denny shuddered. "And the kind of girls I like don't look twice at me."

"Maybe you should try being nice for a change," Lisa said. "And wash your hair once in a while. I know a great shampoo for your hair type."

"Hey, I'm not changing my image for nobody, okay?" Denny said menacingly. Then he softened. "Besides, I met Suki. She's something else."

"I'll say," Zack said under his breath. But somehow, he felt a little sorry for Denny. He wasn't going to destroy the girl of his dreams.

"And she likes me. So I stole some money to buy her a present. But I *did* feel bad about the little guy," he said, pointing at Screech. "I gave the money back, man," Denny said. There was almost a pleading note in his voice.

The gang exchanged glances. "You know," Lisa said, "the children's ward at Palisades General has a storytelling program in the afternoons. People come in and read to the kids. We really need volunteers."

Denny guffawed. "Me with a bunch of rug rats?"

Zack nodded. "That's right, Denny. You with a bunch of rug rats."

"That's our deal," Slater said. "Take it or leave it."

Denny hesitated. "You know, I've always wanted to work with children," he said.

▲　　▼　　▲

Zack was sitting in study hall when he felt a pair of soft hands cover his eyes. He sniffed and smelled baby powder and a light scent of flowers.

"Kelly!" He stood and turned around, and there she was, the old Kelly, dressed in a pink denim miniskirt, flowered T-shirt, and sneakers. "What are you doing here?"

Kelly grinned. "I got kicked out of Miss Fopp's."

"But why?" Zack said, surprised.

"Somebody found your jeans balled up underneath the sofa in the library. They found a receipt for a football video rental, so they knew it was a guy. So they put two and two together and remembered Zackarella Morris getting me out of class. Miss Rumson called Marion, and I was kicked out."

"Kelly, I feel awful," Zack said. "It's all my fault. I'm sorry."

"Are you kidding?" Kelly asked, her blue eyes sparkling. "I'm going to buy you the most deluxe cheeseburger at the Max to thank you. But you'll have to lend me the money. I gave back my allowance to Aunt Marion. Or should I say Mrs. Lenihan."

"Is she really mad at you?" Zack asked.

"Furious," Kelly giggled. "Not only did I sneak a

boy into school, but I skipped the charity fashion show, and I wouldn't make friends with Suki Ballard. But things are going to work out fine for Mrs. Lenihan. She went to a spa in New England for a weekend and discovered a whole tribe of Lenihans in New Hampshire. She's trying out new heirs. It's between an Andrew and a Belinda."

Zack swallowed. "You mean she's not going to put you through school?"

Kelly shook her head happily. "No! Isn't it great? I returned the charm bracelet and the pearls already. And Mr. Vance gave me my job back at the Yogurt 4-U."

"What about your parents?"

"They're happy about it," Kelly said. "They said the money wasn't worth me being miserable. They've been great."

"Wait a second," Zack said, rubbing his head. "Let me get this straight. You mean you're throwing away a chance at all that money? You're not even in the running with Andrew and Belinda?"

"No! I told her I wasn't interested. Isn't it fantastic?" Kelly laughed happily. "I mean, really, Zack. What's being an heiress compared to being plain old Kelly Kapowski at good ol' Bayside High?"

Zack made a strangled sound. He couldn't seem to form words.

Kelly spread her arms to include the Bayside High study hall. "What's millions and millions of dollars compared to all this, Zack? Zack?"

Kelly heard a dull thud. Zack had keeled over in a dead faint. She bent over and fanned him with his notebook. Poor Zack. He must have skipped lunch. As soon as he woke up, she was positive he'd be just as happy about her decision as she was.

Don't miss the next **HOT** novel about the **"SAVED BY THE BELL"** gang

ONE WILD WEEKEND

Zack and the gang head for the mountains for a weekend of romance and excitement. But things get totally out of control when Kelly, Lisa, and Jessie fall head over heels for three gorgeous Italians, and Zack finds himself in more trouble than ever!

Will the girls leave their Bayside boys for charming, European hunks? Can Zack scam his way out of this mess? Find out in the next "Saved by the Bell" novel.